TWO SWORDS
AGAINST ONE

Ty-Sun saw a barred door, and in front of it two guards.

Their bodies were human, but they had the heads of cobras. Emerald pebbly skin drew tautly across narrow skulls. Their eyes were yellow with a black slit at the center. Their reptilian lips twisted into smiles as they drew their swords.

Two against one, but Ty-Sun had no choice. For Blessing, alive or dead, was behind the door . . .

The Black Jade Road

Book Two of
The Land of
Ten Thousand Willows

Ace Books by Kathryn Grant

THE PHOENIX BELLS
THE BLACK JADE ROAD

THE LAND OF TEN THOUSAND WILLOWS

A Fantasy of a China That Never Was

BOOK II:

The Black Jade Road

BY

Kathryn Grant

ACE BOOKS, NEW YORK

This book is an Ace
original edition, and
has never been previously
published.

THE BLACK JADE ROAD

An Ace Book / published by arrangement with
the author

PRINTING HISTORY
Ace edition / March 1989

ISBN: 0-441-06611-9

Ace Books are published by The Berkley Publishing Group,
200 Madison Avenue, New York, New York 10016.
The name "ACE" and the "A" logo are
trademarks belonging to Charter Communications, Inc.

PRINTED IN THE UNITED STATES OF AMERICA

10 9 8 7 6 5 4 3 2 1

For
Emily and Ian,
with love

Lament

The silken song of night-birds awaken me;
    wrapped in my cloak, I gaze at the autumn moon.
How long, how long, I hear the birds cry,
    before I see my beloved home again.

Battles are fought, and many friends lost;
    wearily I travel along the Black Jade Road.
How long, how long, I hear the birds weep,
    before I return home once more.

Sorrow pools in my heart, and I lay awake
    until the moon melts into the dawn.
Though I have come ten thousand li,
    my journey does not end tomorrow.

EMPEROR TY-SUN

Author's Note

Sun, as in the name Ty-Sun, is pronounced "Soon."

Shou is pronounced to rhyme with "how."

A *li* measures approximately one-third of a mile.

Prologue

Across the world, many thousands of miles distant from the Willow Garden, the One watches and envies and hates. There, in the land where it is always spring, the last magical elements of Earth, the dragons, have fled for protection. While they still live, while they flourish, these dragons of old, the Darkness cannot prevail.

And so the Watcher broods, and bides.

PART I

1633

1

Lightning glimmered on the horizon, thunder muttered indistinctly as a burst of wind brought a spattering of cold rain.

Soon the storm will break, Ty-Sun thought wearily as he rubbed a trembling hand across his face, and who knew then what would happen to him and the others remaining in his charge?

In the faint light of early morning, the young Emperor of the Land of Ten Thousand Willows glanced beyond the stern of *The Water Dragon*. In the distance he glimpsed the white sails of the ships which had pursued them since leaving the London docks.

His was only one ship, swift as a dragonfly across the surface of a lily pond, while those of the enemy numbered a handful and thus were unable to maneuver as quickly. Surely his junk would outrun the others; surely Huang Di, the Count of the Wind, would be kind to Ty-Sun and his friends.

He was not as favorably disposed toward the god as he once would have been. The gods of the Land of Ten Thousand Willows had not been kind since he ventured beyond the boundaries of his own land. Before embarking on his quest, he had enjoyed the company of the many gods and goddesses and had performed numerous feats of sorcery

with their approval and encouragement. Moreover, whenever Ty-Sun had called them, the deities had responded by
appearing and aiding him however they might. That had
stopped once he left the Willow Garden. From that moment
on, he could not depend upon the help of the gods.

Many times in the past months he had called upon them;
as yet not one had acknowledged, and so he was forced to
resort to his own magical skills. Luckily, each time his
powers had been sufficient to see them through the various
dangers.

Overhead the red and gold sails billowed outward as the
wind rushed into them. The wind shifted slightly, and all
too quickly the fragile material slacked. Even the red
standard with its gold dragon sewn upon it now hung
limply. He murmured silently, and the hardy silk sails filled
once more. He smiled slightly, then glanced around the
deck of *The Water Dragon*, his expression fading as he
studied the scars from battles past. She had once been sister
to six others, the flagship among his small, proud fleet at
the outset of his journey. Seven exquisite junks, especially
constructed of camphorwood, with teakwood decks and
masts, fittings of polished brass, and intricately carved
figureheads.

The Phoenix, *The Partridge Sky*, *The Moth*, *The Hum-
mingbird*, *The Red Willow Dream*, and *The Jade Butterfly*.
All the ships and their crews and passengers were gone
now; only his *Water Dragon* remained to take him and his
bride and a few comrades home.

A line from an old poem came to mind then: *The sorrows
that cause a heart to grieve.*

He had many sorrows, it was true, but did not suffer the
grief alone.

He strode across to the starboard side where Martin

Bleeker leaned against the railing, staring disconsolately into the water.

Ty-Sun shared his deep sorrow, for only a few hours before, when the first light of the day had scarcely tinted the sky, they had lost a woman they both loved, loved in different ways.

He had lost his favorite concubine; Martin had lost a love just found.

Was it only the night before, Ty-Sun marvelled sadly, that he and his friends had attended the magnificent ball given by King Charles and Queen Henrietta Maria in his honor?

There he and General Soong Kee Yang tested each Englishwoman to ascertain who would be Ty-Sun's empress; a prophecy at his birth twenty-five years ago foretold that he must find a wife before three years had elapsed from the death of his father. After Ty-Sun had ascended the Dragon Throne, he had enjoyed his easy life and had become complacent and heavy in mind and body with rich wines and sugared delicacies. When Soong had come to him nearly a year ago to say he must soon seek a wife, Ty-Sun had ignored him. Finally the general had convinced him to hunt for a consort outside of the Willow Garden, and so his search commenced.

It had ended when the Puritan girl, Blessing Dunncaster, stepped forward. Ty-Sun had met and fallen in love with her several weeks earlier, but even he knew that sentiment did not always enter into a marriage. So she must be tested as had the other women. She held the dragonleaf as it glowed, and in that moment Ty-Sun knew and was overjoyed that she was destined to be his empress. Yet even as she urged him to return to his land that faced a grave danger, armed men broke into the ballroom and attacked them.

Ty-Sun, Soong, Martin and Lord Elphinstone, Martin's master, had fought desperately with the enemy—men who hated Ty-Sun and wished to stop him from taking a wife—while the concubine Spring Rain had hurried Blessing back to *The Water Dragon*. Only after setting sail did they discover—too late—that the young girl was fatally wounded while protecting Blessing. Minutes later the concubine died.

To what fate were they sailing now? he pondered. Shortly afterward, they discovered they were being pursued by the Puritans, that they would not be allowed to leave peacefully, he understood now. Also, Blessing refused to speak to him, blaming him for her brother's death as well as her father's. He had killed her father but surely only through plain self-defense. The man had threatened him, and Ty-Sun had had no choice but to raise his sword, Dragon's Tongue.

As for her brother . . . he didn't know. There had been too much confusion, too many opponents rushing toward him to account for each man there. He agonized over that, too, because he had no wish to kill any member of her family, but her own relatives had raised weapons against him and would have gladly kept her from his side by killing him.

There had been no choice.

What of his friends' injuries? He regarded Martin, whose young face had already aged years in the past few hours. He knew the boy had come on this journey only because of his love for Spring Rain, and now she was gone. Well, he'd do what he could for the lad; he knew Martin would serve him faithfully.

Martin did not speak, and Ty-Sun gently patted the boy's arm.

His faithful adviser Soong was only slightly injured, with a minor gash on the neck which would soon heal, and one side of his long drooping moustache was singed so that he now looked oddly unbalanced. Ty-Sun knew Soong would soon be his old self. Most of the remaining members of his entourage had died at the hands of the Puritans, but Fray Esteban Xavier Navarro Villadiego had miraculously escaped capture and death and had made his way safely back to the junk.

What of himself? he wondered for the first time. His injuries were no more than scratches, he suspected, and yet he suffered—now that he had found his empress, and loved her, she would not have him. If only he could win her over.

A movement along one side caught his attention as Fray Villadiego joined him at the railing. The priest, who had come to the Willow Garden to establish a church and convert the Garden's inhabitants, unsuccessfully so far, had gladly volunteered for this journey with Ty-Sun, and it was amazing he wasn't dead as well, the emperor reflected bitterly.

"Are you injured, Your Majesty?" The Jesuit's voice reflected his concern. Slender, with an angular, clean-shaven face, pale skin, and black eyes, he wore the customary black robes of a priest of the Society of Jesus, and a large silver crucifix hung around his neck. His age was difficult to pinpoint, although Ty-Sun guessed he was in his thirties.

For the first time since they had fled London, Ty-Sun became aware of a throbbing in his side. He peered down at the foot-long slash in his robe and realized he'd indeed been injured.

"A slight scratch, nothing more." He saw no blood, but then the material was red. The once-white dragons and pheasants embroidered on his silk robe were now stained grey with dirt and soot.

"Nonetheless, it should be dressed. You would not wish

it infected, as sometimes even a mere scratch proves most troublesome."

"Yes, yes, you are right, I suppose," Ty-Sun murmured slowly.

Suddenly weariness and grief threatened to overwhelm him, and now that he was aware of his wound, the pain seemed to increase by the moment, pulsating with each beat of his heart. Blindly he thrust his arms out, his vision grown hazy from his fatigue as the priest took his arm and guided him toward a crate at the base of a spar where he could sit.

The wind had come up now, and it blew strands of his long hair across his face. For many moments he tried mustering strength enough to raise his hand to push them away. He felt utterly drained. While Villadiego fetched water and bandages, Ty-Sun leaned against the spar and stared up into the sky. Clouds the color of ink flowed toward one another, massed, swept apart, and then boiled back together. And in the center of this impressive sight fire sparked. Fascinated, he gazed at the play of lightning, watching as one branch broke off and hurtled downward.

"Look out, Your Majesty!" Martin grabbed Ty-Sun and wrenched him away from the spot, not an instant before the lightning struck the crate where Ty-Sun had been sitting. Brilliant fire sizzled momentarily then died out, leaving a charred area.

General Soong, his wound being dressed by one of the few remaining soldiers, witnessed the explosion of sparks then pushed the man away and hurried over. "Are you all right?"

Ty-Sun shook his head, clearing it of the cobwebs that had enveloped him so thoroughly in the past few minutes. His lethargy was most unnatural; it must be another tool of the Enemy. No matter how tired, he must always remain alert. For him it was a matter of life or death. He had once believed that he possessed no enemies, but when the bandits attacked the villages on the outskirts of the Willow Garden, and when his own entourage was set upon several times during their journey, he realized otherwise. Indeed, some great Enemy existed . . . somewhere . . . trying to stop and destroy him, his friends and his country, and most of all the dragons that Ty-Sun protected. If the dragons were destroyed, all life on earth as they knew it would cease.

"My Lord?" the general prompted. His dark eyes were less fierce than usual, and his flowing white hair was tangled. He wore brigandine, black velvet lined with small iron plates. The shoulder pieces were fashioned as gilded dragons with four claws, the five-clawed dragon being the emperor's own symbol. Several ivory buttons which fastened the shoulder and arm pieces together were missing, and his black leather boots looked worn. He still wore *hu sin king*, or Mirror guarding heart, circular plates of white metal with ornamental borders worn across the breast and back of his armor. Beneath the armor he wore a black tunic and trousers.

"Yes, I am fine. Thanks to the quick actions of Martin here." He nodded while the young man reddened to the roots of his brown hair. Not yet twenty years of age, Martin had a square, honest face, large blue eyes fringed with dark lashes, and a slightly large nose. His short hair curled on the edges, although he spent much time tugging futilely at it. The fingers of his square hands were long and capable. He stood on the short side but was muscular and slim, and the new blue jacket and breeches selected especially for the previous night's ball were badly stained. "Thank you, boy, for you have saved my life."

Martin muttered something which might have been a "You're welcome, your lordship," but Ty-Sun couldn't be sure.

Soong was preparing to speak again when Fray Villadi-ego returned on deck and seeing the huddle of men, hurried over.

"What's happened here?"

"The Emperor was nearly struck by lightning," Soong explained. "Martin saved him, though."

"Madre de Dios," the priest whispered as he hastily crossed himself. His eyes narrowed as he stared at Martin. "You must take far more care, Your Majesty." Villadiego set the basin of water down. "You could easily have been killed!"

"Yes, I know," Ty-Sun said, his tone ironic. Soong scowled thoughtfully.

The priest pushed aside the torn material and stared with concern at the eight-inch gash in Ty-Sun's side. It was neither superficial nor one which would cause death, yet it needed tending. Carefully he washed the dried blood from the area, noting that his charge only winced once, then bandaged it so the silk of Ty-Sun's robes would not rub against it.

Instinctively the men ducked as more lightning crackled overhead. At once thunder followed, booming so loudly the deck underfoot shook with the reverberations. The wind moaned forlornly through the ropes and sails, and the ship creaked in counterpoint as it pitched wildly from side to side.

"I don't like this one bit," Soong said, stroking the unscathed side of his moustache as he scowled at the roiling clouds overhead. "This storm is far too convenient, if you ask me. It blew in hardly before we had left London. I smell dark sorcery here."

Silently Ty-Sun agreed. He knew that storms of this magnitude were common in this area and at this time of year, but this bore the distinct mark of the Enemy. Since the

Puritans that the Enemy had sent against him and his friends had failed last night, then something else must be sent to stop them.

Nothing, not even this storm, would stop them now, he resolved. He would survive, as would his friends. Somehow.

"We should go below," Soong yelled over the howling wind. "It's safer." He watched the pursuing ships; they were no closer than before. The wind was working against them as well.

Ty-Sun nodded and beckoned to the others, who followed him below.

Blessing was there, the black and white cat curled up and dozing on her lap. She peeked up only briefly then away, and it was the emptiness in her green eyes that brought further sorrow to Ty-Sun. He started toward her, then stopped. There was nothing he could say to her yet. The time wasn't right—nor did he desire an audience for what he wanted to tell her.

He went to his quarters, and because none of his personal servants had survived the Puritans' attack in the English palace, he changed his clothes by himself for the first time in his life. It was an odd feeling, he thought as he carefully rolled the torn robe up to be thrown out then selected another one, also of red silk. The long sleeves were edged with dragons in gold thread, while one large dragon in emerald silk was appliqued upon the chest.

Truly an emperor's raiments, and yet the emperor must play servant as well. He smiled slightly. The emperor must learn many things during this trip; duties he never suspected he would have to do. So far it had proved beneficial.

As an afterthought, he also pulled on a pair of black trousers and leather boots like those Soong wore then belted the robe with a cord of black silk. He was doing things that a year earlier would have been absolutely unthinkable, and now that he was doing them, he didn't mind. Not as much as he'd once believed he would, so long ago.

He caught his reflection in the mirror above his bed. The soft round face familiar for so long had been replaced by a much leaner one. For the first time in his life, he saw his cheekbones, knife-sharp against the outline of his face, and marvelling, he brushed them lightly with his fingers. The delicate sheaths of silver which protected his fingernails clicked, a sound barely heard over the wind's keening.

Gold flecked his deepset, rust-brown eyes, and his shoulder-length hair, black and quite straight, needed brushing. The pins once restraining it were missing and he observed with faint amusement that he needed a shave. Who now would perform this delicate job? He regarded the long sheaths on his nails and doubted this was a skill he could learn easily, much less accomplish without minor bloodshed.

He was the One-True and August Emperor and Magician of the Land of Ten Thousand Willows, Lord of the Sun and the Moon, Son of Heaven, Bearer of the Star Wand, Holder of the Lotus, Guardian of the Dragons of Earth, Protector of Long Life, Wielder of Dragon's Tongue, Warlord of the Wall of Living Stone, Scholar, Poet, Painter, and Dutiful Son of the late Ty-Ch'an, and tonight as well he played the servant. He was amused by the thought, surely absurd more than a year before.

He stared into the depths of the small, sandalwood casket containing the jewels he had brought—far too many, he realized now—then finally selected a long strand of clear amber beads. His people considered amber to be the soul of the tiger transformed into mineral after death. It was a symbol of courage and was also an amulet against evil, and for some reason he suspected he would need such an item soon.

Ty-Sun left his quarters and found Martin in the small galley fixing dinner with Blessing helping him. They soon sat down for a modest meal of stew, bread, and English ale, and although many long hours had passed since they'd last eaten, only Soong displayed much appetite. He ate with his usual gusto, for having long been a soldier, he knew hardships meant intermittent meals and was determined to leave no food uneaten.

Afterward, without another word, Blessing returned to her small quarters across from those of Ty-Sun. Fray Villadiego also retired to his quarters for prayers and meditation and bowed low to Ty-Sun and the general before leaving.

Ty-Sun pushed away from the table and Ch'u, the small grey-brown dog with the large eyes that he had brought along for company, lay at his feet. He needed to talk with Soong about their plans.

Just then the general returned to sit alongside Ty-Sun. "I fed the bear." He referred to the immense brown bear Ty-Sun had rescued during their unsuccessful stay in Russland. "He isn't very happy about this storm, Your Majesty."

"Nor am I. I think I must stay alert tonight, old friend. I think the Enemy will move against us during the storm."

"I'll take first watch then," Soong volunteered promptly.

"I the second," said Martin, listening from the shadows.

"You're a good man, Martin, and I am pleased you elected to come with us."

"If possible, sir, my lord," the boy stumbled a bit over his words, "I would like to serve you. The way I did Lord Elphinstone. That is, if you'll have me." These last words rushed out in a jumble as a slow blush crept into his face.

Ty-Sun inclined his head. "I would be honored, Martin." He glanced back at the old warrior. "I will take the third one then, and as for the fourth, who will take that watch?"

"The priest," Soong said bluntly. "Let him work for his meals."

Soong mistrusted the Jesuit and never hesitated to let Ty-Sun know that. Spring Rain had disliked the priest, too. For some time Ty-Sun had thought his friends cared little for the man's religion but now understood that wasn't so. He was intrigued by the Spaniard but wasn't sure now if he could completely trust him, not the way he did Martin. Still, Soong was right; the priest should take his turn as well.

"Very well."

"I'll go tell the father." Martin nodded once to them, and then they were alone.

Ty-Sun took a deep breath, then sighed, aware that Soong watched him closely. "I'm glad you weren't injured severely, my old friend."

"Not as much as I, Your Majesty! And what of your wound?"

He gestured, dismissing the other's concern. "It's very slight. And I'm sure it will heal within days. Think nothing of it."

"It isn't that which preys upon your mind."

The general's eyes were shrewd, sometimes too shrewd, Ty-Sun mused.

"No. I keep thinking of poor Spring Rain and her last moments alive."

"She died for you, my lord—protecting the woman you love. She would have wished it no other way."

"But, I do. Why must she die, Soong? Poor Martin loved her, and in time I think she would have loved him; that's why he chose to come with us, and now she is taken from him."

"He has found another lord to serve, though, and that will give him purpose."

"Perhaps."

"There is more then."

"Yes."

"The girl?"

Ty-Sun nodded. The girl. Blessing Dunncaster, the woman he loved, the woman who had held the dragonleaves and who had heard the voices of the dragons. The woman whose family he had helped kill and who now despised him above all else.

"What am I to do? She hates me."

"Wait," Soong counseled. "Give her time to grieve over her family, as you must have time to grieve for Spring Rain and the loss of the others. Time will heal her wounds—as well as yours—and then you must set about wooing her."

"How?"

"That, my friend," the general said with a knowing nod, "is something you must figure out by yourself. No one can help you there."

Ty-Sun sighed. More puzzles. "I'm afraid you might be right."

"On this matter, I know I am."

"Time, then, and patience. I fear it is something I've never been very good at. Ah well, I am learning many virtues on this journey."

They chatted about their plans, then when Soong went to watch, Ty-Sun returned to his quarters and lay down upon the narrow bed. He closed his eyes but did not sleep. He did not think sleep would come. There was too much to consider.

2

The emperor was ambling past the aloe-wood pavilion with
its bamboo trellises, along the paths between the immacu-
late beds of irises and peonies, nodding purple and scarlet
and gold in the afternoon sunlight, and the air was fragrant
with the scent of thousands of blooms. He gazed around at
the imperial gardens, stretching for many *li*, and smiled
with contentment.

Ty-Sun loved them all, these beautiful flowers and trees
and shrubs, and the reflecting ponds built around them. He
enjoyed promenades through the gardens or just sitting on a
marble bench and closing his eyes. He found peace here.

Willow branches trailed gracefully along the mirror-like
surfaces of the ponds, and pausing by one, he gazed into its
depths. Dozens of tiny fish flashed gold and silver and
bronze then were gone, and the water shimmered strangely
as if something larger, something not of the pond, had
disturbed it. Momentarily his smile disappeared. But the
water had already calmed again, and his smile returned.

He followed the twisting path of red and white marble
leading to the Tower of Beautiful Views and entered
through the lacquered door. He climbed up the steps slowly,
not bothering to count them as he had done so carefully as
a child, and when he gained the top, he gazed out over the
imperial city.

The buildings—houses and theaters and temples and schools—gleamed white in the sunlight, the red-tiled roofs shimmering. The green of tiny gardens and parks dotted the city like a patchwork, and he watched the city's residents hurry down Bronze Camel Avenue and Green Jasper Terrace and the adjoining streets. He watched as horses and camels and asses and other beasts of burden made their way toward the markets, their masters and mistresses at their sides urging them onward.

Faintly he heard the shrill cries of the street vendors, pushing through the crowds with their wondrous wares and grinned as children sat enthralled, watching a puppet show. Somewhere on the palace grounds someone was singing. He recognized the lilting tune as "The Snapped Willow."

His people, his city. He loved them and knew they loved and worshipped him.

A very benign relationship.

Yet something wasn't right; he could sense it, a disturbance in the air. Almost as if the day were somehow not right, as if—

Ty-Sun blinked.

Most of the sunlight had faded from the sky, the roofs now tinted with purple, and it was close to evening. Had he fallen asleep? How long had he been here? Far too long.

Uneasy, he whirled around quickly, but he was alone in the tower. He tapped fingers along the wall, listening to the click of the silver nail sheaths. He thought someone was watching him, but when he stared down at the city, it was as it should be. Life went on, men and women busy with their own concerns.

And yet—what?

He gazed around, briefly looking at the three other palace towers, deserted now at this advanced hour. To the south of the island on which the city was built lay Wilderness Wood, but nothing moved there, at least nothing his eyes could detect.

To the north and east he saw the stones leading to the First Emperor's tomb. Nothing stirred there. Ty-Sun surveyed Nine Dragon Bridge leading to Dragon's Wander, the timeless sanctuary of the dragons. Nothing seemed wrong there, but it had been some time since he'd visited. He should go there now. Perhaps they would sooth him; perhaps they would erase this feeling of great unease.

He hurried down out of the tower and back into the palace, ably dodging concubines and government officials and nobles who all desired speaking with him about urgent matters until he was at last alone in his bedchamber. Along one wall was a black lacquered door; he was the only one who held a key to its lock. Not even his father had known of this secret way.

Beyond the door was a tunnel lined with dark terra cotta tiles that passed under the palace and the city to the other side of the walls. There it opened into bushes thick with crimson flowers smelling of vanilla that concealed the entrance.

It was dark now as he crossed Nine Dragon Bridge, his footsteps echoing on the marble. Mist rose in great clouds, surrounding him, as he stepped into the bamboo groves that flourished on the island. He passed the ruins of Green Dragon Turret and thought of his previous visit to the island. He had come at last to Dragon's Wander shortly before starting his journey.

His journey.

His brow furrowed with concentration. There was something important that he must remember. Something about the journey, but the thought, as quickly as a silver fish, slipped away from him.

Ancient almond trees grew gnarled, their grey branches

bending this way and that, and moss like filmy silks, hung from the bark. The short avenue paved with broken stone, its sides lined with statues of serpents and tigers and camels and lions, seemed slick underfoot, and he paused to inspect the moisture. It hadn't rained, and this substance wasn't dew. He stooped, touching it with his hand, then smelled the dampness on his fingers.

A familiar scent, but one he couldn't place offhand. Quickly wiping his hand on his robes, he went farther into the marshy land. He was waiting to hear the phoenix bells, the high-pitched trilling of the dragons that greeted him when he visited.

Tonight he heard nothing but the wind soughing through branches and the creaking of the bamboo.

His pace quickened. He called the dragons by name, but none answered.

He stepped off the path into the bamboo where the dragons customarily slept.

"Madame Shou?"

She was the oldest of the dragons, a scarred veteran of battles long ago in England where she'd lived before fleeing to the Willow Garden, and she was one of his favorites. Tonight, though, unlike a hundred times before, she did not respond.

Cold seized him as he leaned down to examine something white in the faint light.

Bones.

With an astonished cry, he stood up. A pile of bones that could only belong to a dragon.

And beyond that a small carcass, its gold and crimson skin peeled back, revealing reddened muscles and tendons. One of the younger dragons. As a child of eight, Ty-Sun had named him Jin Feng, or Golden Wind.

Beyond lay Snowblossom, killed the same way, and tiny

Willow Drum, who looked as if all the blood was drained from her body. Past those two, he found still more bodies. Some were burned beyond recognition, some carved like roasted meat, others dead through dismemberment or slashed throats.

Dead.

All of them.

Numbly he passed the bodies, so still in the night, until he came upon Madame Shou. The tears in his eyes overflowed now.

She had been impaled. Her great wings hung limp, broken, drooping across the ground, and he saw their delicate membranes had been deliberately trampled. Her eyes had been gouged out, her claws ripped out one by one. Weeping, he petted her huge and bloodied head; she was already cool.

He stared dazed at the carnage. He was sick to his stomach, stunned by the death, and blindly he stumbled out of the bamboo.

Who could have done this terrible thing? And why? Why, he asked himself as he ran down the avenue to the bridge. Why?

On the bridge, he paused and sighted the birds of carrion hovering overhead, and he fled to the palace, the safety of his bedchamber.

When he had returned and closed and locked the black door and leaned against it, his breath spent, his heart pounding, he knew who had murdered the dragons.

The Enemy.

The Enemy had come to the Land of Ten Thousand Willows to murder his charges. If the Enemy could harm the dragons, then he could just as well come after Ty-Sun or anyone else in the Palace.

He would be waiting.

❈— 3 —❈

Ty-Sun awoke from the nightmare disoriented. He had dreamed he was in the Willow Garden once more, and he had crossed Nine Dragon Bridge to Dragon's Wander, and there he found—

In the darkness of his cabin he shuddered, remembering discovering the bodies of his beloved dragons, remembering the terrible sight.

But, he told himself, it was only a dream; nothing more. And yet.

Something was wrong; he sensed that the way he had in the dream. Something was very wrong, and as he sat up and swung his legs over the side of the bed, he knew what it was.

The floor of his cabin was tilted at such an angle he could scarcely sit up. He heard a low whining, and perplexed, he leaned down carefully and peered under the bed. Ch'u had slid there and was lodged against the wall, now so slanted it could have been the floor, and could not move. Laughing slightly, Ty-Sun grabbed the dog, pulling him out. Gratefully Ch'u licked his face then barked once.

"I know a good place for you, my friend," Ty-Sun said as he straightened precariously. He slipped the small dog into a voluminous pocket then stroked the silky head. Ch'u would be safe there.

25

The floor slipped a little more, and Ty-Sun clutched the frame of his bed so he wouldn't fall over. Now, for the first time, he noticed the noise. How could he ever have slept through it? he wondered. The wind shrieked and howled, sputtered and bellowed like demonic spirits, while the ship plunged and tossed upon the waves as if weighing no more than a cork.

Over the wind he heard the sailors shouting on deck. He couldn't make out the words, but heard the panic in their voices.

Ty-Sun edged across the cabin, hanging onto various things, until he was at the door then opened it carefully. On the same side as his bed, it fell open with a bang, and he nearly tumbled out into the main cabin. Martin was there, a trifle sleepy in the light of the wildly swaying lantern.

"What's happened?" Ty-Sun demanded. "Whose watch is it?"

"The priest's," Soong said from the shadows. He poked his head out of a corner where he'd apparently slid moments before.

"The third watch was mine."

Soong shrugged casually. "I decided to let you sleep, Your Majesty, and had the priest watch instead. I awoke much as I imagine you did."

A muffled roar came from another corner, and Ty-Sun saw the trembling muzzle of the bear. Soong must have let him out. Good.

"What of Blessing?"

"I am here." It was the first she'd spoken since accusing him of being a murderer. She stood close to Martin, and in her arms she clutched the cat, as if afraid to let go. The faint light gave her a pale appearance, as if she'd been weeping.

Ty-Sun nodded. "Good. And what of the priest? Has anyone been outside?"

"He hasn't come back yet. I glanced outside momentarily, but the wind's too fierce, and I didn't get a proper look. If we go out on deck, we'll tie ropes around our waists to link us together. I don't want any of us washed overboard."

"I'll go," Martin offered.

"And I," Ty-Sun said.

Soong prepared to protest, then thought better of it and snapped his mouth shut. He merely nodded. He knew there was no dissuading Ty-Sun once the emperor's mind was made up.

The men found some sturdy rope coiled in a wooden cabinet overhead and knotted one end firmly to Martin's waist, then played out a generous length and tied Ty-Sun.

"I'll secure it to something solid in here first," Soong yelled, "and will hold onto it, just in case. You must help me, Mistress Blessing. I'm strong, but I need your strength as well." She nodded wordlessly. "It's the only way we can keep from losing them."

"I'm ready," Ty-Sun shouted over the constant racket of the wind. He detected another sound, too, which he identified as rain, but certainly this was no gentle, lulling shower. This was a driving, crashing downpour, the sort of rain that destroyed, not nurtured.

Briefly he wondered what course the wind had blown *The Water Dragon* onto these past few hours, and he prayed the junk would hold to its name and come through the storm safely.

Martin climbed up the stairway that lay nearly sideways now, then, putting his shoulder against the wood, pushed the hatch open. It flew away with a crash as buckets of water, both from the sea and the skies, poured in and drenched him.

"Well, it's a wet one out there, that's for sure," the

young man said half to himself and taking a deep breath and pushing the hair out of his eyes, climbed through the hatch.

Ty-Sun followed. At that moment he remembered little Ch'u still in his pocket, and then it was too late to turn back. The world he entered was a nightmare. *The Water Dragon* was nearly on her starboard side, her spars broken in pieces, her sails ripped, some swept away. In this dark world above deck, rain and seawater and wind slashed at him, whipped away his breath, and within seconds he was soaking wet. His hair plastered across his face, he staggered after Martin.

"Do you see anything?" Ty-Sun shouted. He tried standing, but the fierceness of the wind forced him into a semicrouch.

"No-o-o."

Even though he wasn't far from the young Englishman, he heard the boy's words only faintly and could see him dimly.

A monstrous wave crashed over the side of the junk, smashing against Ty-Sun and nearly knocking him off his feet. He grabbed onto another hatch, yet closed, and clung tightly. Behind him the rope tightened.

Underfoot the deck was slippery and slimy, as though the sea had thrown its very dregs upon the ship, and their footing, always precarious, changed constantly. The deck convulsed and buckled beneath them, sometimes rearing up unexpectedly. It was a struggle, too, for both men to stand against the force of the gale wind and the heaving waves. The thunder pounded closer, shaking them with its strength, and even the lightning seemed only a few paces away.

Ty-Sun thought a moon rode high in the sky, but nothing of it could be detected through the black, rolling clouds. White lightning, forked and deadly, burst overhead, and in that moment he scanned the deck. He glimpsed several of

Soong's soldiers, but most of the men, lashed to spars and railings, were dead.

Drowned, he reflected grimly, or struck by lightning. He saw nothing on the deck beyond Martin and himself, and he wondered what had happened to the sailors. And to the priest. Had they all been washed overboard, or had they somehow managed to seek shelter in another part of the junk?

"Father!" Martin called, his hands cupped. "Father Villadiego."

A faint sound almost covered by the deafening thunder issued from their right, and with difficulty the two men crept toward it. They found a young soldier whom Ty-Sun recognized as a member of Soong's elite. He had lashed himself to a railing, but as more lightning lit the deck, Ty-Sun and Martin saw he was dying. Part of the railing had split off, impaling him.

"My lord," he whispered, recognizing Ty-Sun as he raised pain-dulled eyes. "My lord."

Ty-Sun caressed the soldier's head briefly, and even as he did so the boy died.

"I don't see the priest."

"Nor I, Your Majesty. I think we'd best go back," Martin shouted while Ty-Sun nodded.

The air was thick with the ozone of the lightning and the slimy smell of the sea plus the bitter scent of death and despair. Wave after wave crashed across the deck, pulling away more bodies, more timber.

With tears in his eyes, Ty-Sun gazed slowly about at the wreckage. Gone was the proud junk, last of his fleet of seven sparkling ships. Gone were the courtiers and his concubine and his soldiers and sailors. All gone to their deaths.

A piece of panelling nearly the size of a man was sucked

up by the wind. For a moment it whirled around, then flew straight toward Ty-Sun. He tried ducking but was far too slow. The panelling slammed against his forehead, and he blinked as everything around him blazed silver and black and red. He slid down onto the deck, heard the muffled protest of Ch'u, and was drifting off into unconsciousness, when he heard a shriek. Reflexively he grabbed for the rope in front of him to pull the boy toward him, but the rope was loose. He stared at the ragged end.

Martin had been swept away.

Ty-Sun blinked and shook his head, trying to ignore the pain rippling through him. He must find the boy. With difficulty he heaved himself to his feet and through the bloody haze veiling his eyes, glanced around the ruined deck. The ship shuddered, and he was thrown forward, farther away from the hatch. He rose once more, and toward the bow he caught a glimpse of Martin, hanging desperately to a crate nearly his size which had not yet been dislodged.

Little by little Ty-Sun, sometimes stopping to breath deeply and dab the blood from his eyes, eased forward on the wet surface until he could stretch out an arm and reach the Englishman.

Martin's lips moved in silent prayer, and his eyes were squeezed shut against what he suspected would be his fate, and so he hadn't seen the other's approach.

"Grab on!" Ty-Sun shouted, and Martin's eyes opened, and he stared in shock. He knew the boy probably thought he was imagining things. "Grab my hand!"

Martin strained, and his fingers brushed the tips of Ty-Sun's.

"You must let go!"

Martin nodded to let Ty-Sun know he understood, and as he cautiously let go of the crate, he pushed forward until the emperor clasped his wrists, and then agonizingly slowly he was being pulled toward the other man.

When Martin lay alongside him, Ty-Sun shouted, "Follow the rope back to the hatch. Go below."

Martin nodded and wrapping one arm around the rope, inched toward the hatch. Ty-Sun glanced back just in time to see the boy tumble below deck.

Wearily he cradled his head on his arms. This was the only way he could breathe easily; the wind was so strong it just whipped his breath away, and he needed to rest for a moment before he made his way back. He was tired, so very tired, and the blood still gushed from the cut in his forehead. He felt it with his fingertips, felt the stickiness and then wiped it on the wooden deck.

He must go now. Soong and the others would help him once he returned. He reached for the rope to guide him along and saw it lay slack. As the rain continued hammering at him, he jerked the rope toward him; the other end was frayed through.

He had no way of getting back.

The ship rose high on the crest of a wave, and Ty-Sun, grimly rising, started toward the hatch. At that very moment the junk flipped onto the port side, and with frustration, Ty-Sun realized he was sliding farther away from the hatch.

His back slammed against a railing, and he bit back the cry of pain. The wood behind him buckled, held momentarily, then gave way, and he was tumbling into the dark depths of the waters.

As he was swept away from the junk, he sighted a black form looming on the deck nearby. He squinted at it through the rain and realized it was a dog, its eyes blazing like dying embers—like the dog in the London palace gardens that had threatened him. But that couldn't be. The only dog onboard was Ch'u, and he was still in the pocket. Where had that dog come from?

Then the hound leaped into the swirling water and was gone.

Ty-Sun breathed deeply, inhaled water, and blackness enveloped him.

4

Something warm and wet and not altogether unpleasant rasped against the side of his face.

Keeping his eyes shut because he was dreaming of jade flutes and pipes of gold and of an immense banquet fit only for an emperor, Ty-Sun wiggled his nose as if that simple action would make the irritant go away.

When the warm and wet thing persisted, he tried brushing it away with a hand. He didn't want to lose a single moment of the dream; he'd been about to sample the chrysanthemum wine. But his arm wouldn't respond, and he realized then it was trapped under his body.

As he tried dislodging his arm, he also became aware that he was wet, in fact, completely soaked through to the skin and that his cheek seemed embedded in a gritty substance. The thing touching his face snuffled now and sneezed upon him as well.

He opened his eyes and stared sideways into the moist brown eyes of Ch'u.

Ty-Sun lay on his stomach, his cheek against sand, and his clothes were heavy with water. He scowled, trying to remember how he came to be here—wherever that was— then the memory flooded back in an instant as he recalled the terrible storm and how the rope had snapped and he had fallen overboard.

Ch'u licked him again.

The dog, its head cradled between extended paws, barked as Ty-Sun reached out to him.

"Good boy." The croaking issuing from his throat was scarcely recognizable as his own voice. He must have swallowed a lot of sea water. He coughed, wincing at the rasp in his throat.

It was a miracle the little dog had freed himself from Ty-Sun's pocket and survived drowning. But what of the others?

The sun hung straight overhead, and as he sat up somewhat groggily and gazed around, he saw he'd been lying along a narrow strand of sand with the water lapping at his feet. To the left lay the sea, along his right a line of sand dunes interspersed with what looked like manmade stone walls.

Was this England? Surely *The Water Dragon* hadn't been blown back to the land they had been fleeing. But if not England, what land was it? And where were the others?

Slowly he got to his feet, and Ch'u, thinking his master wanted to play, barked and jumped from one paw to the other.

"Hush," he commanded softly, his throat feeling somewhat better this time, although he still swallowed with difficulty. Oh, for a goblet of chrysanthemum wine, he thought wistfully, and for the first time remembered the plank that had knocked him down the night before, right before he slid into the sea.

He raised his fingers, and felt the dried blood on his forehead. The wound throbbed only a little which was good. He frowned, too, recalling the black dog he had seen moments before he had gone under the water. Where had the animal come from? Where was it? Had it been washed up on the shore as well?

As he glanced up and down the length of the beach, he

saw things, dark against the white, dotting it. With weariness as well as his wet clothes weighing him down, he slowly approached the first bit of wreckage with Ch'u eagerly following.

Sunlight glinted off metal, and with great relief, he recognized Dragon's Tongue. He wouldn't have been surprised to discover his sword at the bottom of the sea now with *The Water Dragon*, but somehow it had found its way to its owner. It was a magical weapon, of course, so perhaps he shouldn't have been astonished after all. He strapped it on, then proceeded to see what else the sea had spit up during the night.

He found Soong some yards away, sleeping peacefully on his back at the base of a dune and still clutching a length of rope in one hand. When Ty-Sun knelt and touched his shoulder, the soldier instantly awakened.

"Who else?" Soong asked, as he struggled to sit. "Who else made it?"

"I don't know. I just awoke. Ch'u was washing my face."

Soong looked down at the dog, then grinned. Ty-Sun helped him to his feet.

Ch'u proved the first to find the bear, who'd been thrown easily over an immense sand dune as if he weighed little more than a feather. Curled in a great furry mound, the creature was unconscious, its rasping breath echoing in the silence.

Ty-Sun ordered Ch'u to stay and guard the animal, and as they filed away, he wondered, with a sinking heart, if this was all they would find.

There was no sign of Fray Villadiego or Martin or Blessing, and with each step, he grew more disheartened. Yet he couldn't allow himself to consider the worst. Not yet.

The sun blazed on the sand, its rays sparkling off the quartz in the tiny grains, and they found it difficult to see. Yet they forced themselves to continue with this forbidding task. Up the beach the two men found more wreckage strewn along the bright sand . . . a coiled rope, Soong's bow and whistling arrows, the small sandalwood casket containing Ty-Sun's jewels, various food stores. For the moment, they left it all, except Soong's weapon; they would return later and gather their few belongings together.

As they ranged farther up the beach, neither one speaking, they spotted another person staggering toward them. For a moment Ty-Sun thought it was Blessing, then he realized it was a man. Within minutes he saw it was Martin who, recognizing them, ran to them.

"It's good to see you whole and alive," the general said.

Ty-Sun nodded. "Have you seen Blessing?" he asked finally.

The young man shook his head. He had several bruises along his right cheek, and one eye was discolored and swollen shut.

"No, I haven't, although I did find some supplies we can use."

"Good," said Soong. "Do you see that tall dune down the beach?" Martin nodded. "Bring everything you can down there; we'll make our camp behind it. It'll give us some protection from the sea and anyone—or thing—which might be there. In the meantime, we'll retrace our steps down the beach."

Soong and Ty-Sun headed back down the beach. The sun rapidly dried out Ty-Sun's robes, so he found it more comfortable to walk.

Some distance from where Ty-Sun had awakened, the two men found the Orb of White Jade nearly buried in the sand. Miraculously it had escaped injury, and with great care, Ty-Sun slipped it into the pocket in which he'd put Ch'u the previous night.

They found bodies here, and with his mouth dry, Ty-Sun passed through them, staring down into each bloated face. He recognized them as sailors and did not see Villadiego's body or that of Blessing.

Surely he should feel optimistic, he told himself, when he did not find her body at once. He should, but he couldn't, and as the hours passed, the last hope he'd had flickered and winked out like a candle that had been snuffed.

Martin had finished bringing the supplies to their make-shift camp and now followed behind to help Soong bury the dead while Ty-Sun went on searching. By nightfall, he had not yet found Blessing's body or the priest's, and disheartened, he returned.

"I don't like staying here." Soong stroked his nearly ruined moustache. "The land is by far too flat, and thus any fire we make will be seen. I have no idea of what reception might await us."

"Then what do you suggest?"

"Martin found an abandoned farmhouse not far from here. We should stay there for the night. It'll give us protection from the weather." He scanned the night sky, but no stars could be seen. No clouds scudded across the blackness, and yet he could not forget the savage storm that had so unexpectedly swept them here. He shuddered.

"All right, Soong. We should relocate our supplies there."

"It's already done."

"Good."

The farmhouse wasn't far but was located well away from the dunes and the high stone walls. Once it had been white-washed inside and out, but the elements and years of neglect had long ago discolored it. Inside the floor was sand, once swept smooth, and Ty-Sun found the house built around a small courtyard. In the center stood a well that still worked. The house contained only a few good-sized rooms and a kitchen with a large brick oven and fireplace along one wall. Some pots, now dusty, had been left behind, and Martin busied himself with fixing dinner.

In the room beyond the kitchen Martin and Soong had deposited their few belongings and built a roaring fire in the fireplace there. Here Ty-Sun found the bear now awake, although sporting a bandage about the crown of its head. It grumbled a greeting when it saw him.

He crossed to the bear and patted its solid, furry flank, then picked up Ch'u, who licked his chin, and sat on a low bench beside the fire. Unblinking, he stared at the flickering flames.

"You didn't find her?" Soong asked.

"No."

"Perhaps tomorrow then."

Ty-Sun did not answer, but knew he would not find her tomorrow, or the day after, or the day after that. She was lost to him.

"Did you bury all the bodies?"

Soong nodded. "It took hours, but we finally finished, and then I helped Martin bring the rest of the supplies here. Well, at least for a while, we have shelter and fire, and some food and blankets."

"Food?" For the first time Ty-Sun realized he was hungry; he couldn't remember when he'd last eaten. Oh yes, now he recalled; it had been the meal Martin had prepared the night before, and even then he had not finished the stew.

"Quite a bit of the stores washed ashore," Martin called eagerly from the next room, "and few were ruined, so we salvaged what we could. I'm afraid it's really not much, my lord, though," he said, glancing worriedly in at the emperor.

"It will be fine, I have no doubt," Ty-Sun said with a smile. His face felt stiff, and he had trouble pulling his muscles into expressions. Weariness numbed him, and with fingers which scarcely felt, he ate the simple meal of roasted meat and vegetables that Martin had prepared. "Excellent," he murmured.

Martin had even located some bowls and plates of plain pottery. He filled one and gave it to the bear, who roared its thanks and began noisily eating. Ch'u waited patiently for his master to finish so he might lick the plate.

Soong leaned back on his elbows and stared across at his emperor. The man looked as if he were in shock; his eyes were wide, unblinking; and whenever someone made a noise, he started. Sleep would help, Soong decided, sleep and time. He sighed, wondering what had become of the young girl Ty-Sun loved. Was she dead? Or perhaps worse, had the Enemy captured her? He would not mention that suspicion to his emperor. Some things were better left unsaid.

The three men ate silently, and then while Martin cleaned the dishes and prepared for the first watch, the bear lay down and fell asleep. Ty-Sun lay alongside it, the animal keeping him warm on one side, the fire in front. Soong drew a blanket up over Ty-Sun, who thanked him quietly. Ch'u was already asleep on his back next to his master's chest.

"Did you find the time-telling glass?"

"No." Ty-Sun closed his eyes.

Soong sighed. Before they had departed the Land of Ten Thousand Willows, the emperor had stopped at the gates, and there Sheng-mu, Princess of the Streaked Clouds, had appeared and presented Ty-Sun with an enclosed glass filled with thousands of tiny pearls. Sheng-mu had explained that each pearl, as it dropped, marked the passage of another day.

Already more than two hundred had collected at the bottom of the glass, and now Soong would have to keep track of the days. They could not let them slip past without marking; Ty-Sun must return to the Willow Garden by the third anniversary of his father's death, and he must have his bride with him.

Soong knew they could return fairly easily by that time, except for one rather crucial matter—just as they'd finally located Blessing Dunncaster, they had quickly lost her.

Tomorrow they would devote all day to searching, and then if they did not find her within a week, they must leave. And then they must make their way as quickly as possible home. Was that not what Blessing herself had said?

All too clearly he remembered the night of the ball at the English court, even though the evening seemed to have occurred a century earlier. He had just passed the dragon-leaf to her, and as it glowed within her hands, all in the ballroom heard a rustling sound. Madame Shou, the oldest dragon remaining in the Willow Garden, then appeared overhead.

The girl claimed the dragon brought Ty-Sun a message that he must return home at once because the Garden faced a mortal danger. Then the dragon disappeared, and even as Ty-Sun declared Blessing the woman he had chosen for his empress, the Puritans, swords in their hands, stormed into the ballroom.

Home. As soon as possible.

What was happening in the Willow Garden? The gods alone knew, and they hadn't spoken to Ty-Sun since he'd come west. Soong sighed, and continued staring into the flames.

5

Long after he had retired to his makeshift bed, Ty-Sun lay with his eyes closed and listened to the sounds in the room: the snapping of the flames on the log, the sound of crickets outside, Soong's deep voice grumbling once or twice without words, the bear and Ch'u snoring. He was exhausted, and he knew he needed rest desperately.

But try as he might, sleep would not come, and he tossed uneasily during the night. Once when the wind rose, rattling branches of the trees outside, he thought he heard ever so faintly a woman's voice singing. Blessing, he thought, and his heart pounding wildly, he rose to glance out a window. Then he remembered.

Blessing was lost.

The pain and darkness filled him again, and into that shadow he fell asleep.

The next morning after breakfast, the three survivors took stock of their possessions.

"We can last on these stores for a good week or more," Soong said, eyeing the boxes and crates that Martin had neatly stacked, "but afterward, we'll need to hunt for food—or else make raids."

Ty-Sun lifted an eyebrow. "Raids? Why not go into a town and buy supplies?"

"We don't know where we are yet, and so we don't know if the inhabitants here are friendly."

"Ah yes, general, they might well be in the pay of the Enemy."

"Or under his sway."

"Have you scouted around the area yet?"

"Martin and I rose some hours ago before the sun had come up fully and poked about."

"And?"

"The area isn't completely deserted as I had first thought—and hoped. There are some houses north of us, but not so close they'll notice us. Another farm lies to the south, but it was too distant for me to see anyone moving about."

"Do you have any idea where we might have been tossed ashore?"

"No, Your Majesty, I don't," Soong replied frankly. "I know that we were headed toward France when the storm came upon us, but only the gods know where the winds blew us afterward. We could easily have gone south or north."

"I don't think it's Spain," Martin said, almost apologetically. "It's not hot enough for Spain, which is filled with deserts and high mountains, or so Lord Elphinstone always told me."

"Very good, Martin. I doubt we could have gone any farther south than Spain or Portugal. No, so we must have been blown northward or across to France. Which leaves us where?"

Soong cleared his throat. "Doubtless, Your Majesty, you've noticed the land here is level with the sea, and that this farm is protected from the sea by dunes and stone walls. I know of only one area where that is a common practice. I think we must be in the Netherlands. The south is controlled by the Spanish; as for the north, I know little about it."

"And you don't know if we'll find friends or foes here?"

"No. There is a war going on in these countries, one that has raged for many years. I don't think either side will welcome strangers."

Ty-Sun said nothing.

"Martin and I searched farther up and down the beach. We didn't find Blessing or the priest. Later, when the sun is lower in the sky, we'll search behind the walls and the dunes."

Ty-Sun nodded, but he knew the search would prove futile.

The following morning Soong rose first and without waking the others went outside. He did not like the silence in which Ty-Sun had shrouded himself, and he was determined to find evidence of Blessing—either alive or dead.

He had said they could stay here a week, but now he knew they should leave before then. A week in one place was far too long, especially when the Enemy still might be searching for them, and the longer they remained in one spot, the easier they would be to locate. Also, it was so flat in this part of the country and there were few trees or bushes—thus hiding would be more difficult—and he doubted they would be able to find an abandoned house each time they decided to camp.

Much of the ground around the farmhouse was of a sandy composition, and for the first time he observed the soft impressions there. There were two sets of tracks, one human, one not, and his lips puckered slightly and stroked the singed half of his moustache. He went inside to check the stores and found several items missing.

He followed the tracks away from the farmhouse through

a marshy area toward a small abandoned building. He and Martin had searched it the day before, but that didn't mean someone wasn't living there now.

He tried keeping his approach quiet, but it was difficult as he knew she must be watching him. He could feel unseen eyes on him, and he did not think they were those of the Enemy. When he stood not far from the small building, he stopped.

"Blessing," he called, his voice soft. He didn't want to sound harsh or commanding, but he knew she was there. "Blessing, it's General Soong. You don't have to hide any longer."

Here the ground became rocky and hard, and he could no longer trace the footprints, but he was convinced she had come here. He waited, and when she did not answer, he sighed deeply and called her name again.

A faint movement from his left, and the old general turned. She stood by the side of the building, and he suspected she had come out a back way. He did not move immediately; he did not want to frighten her. He caught a glimpse of the black and white cat as it rubbed itself against her ankles.

How they had both survived he didn't know, but thank the gods for that. Her hair was no longer neatly brushed, and it flowed thickly about her shoulders in a red torrent that caught the rays of the morning sun. He thought it a far more attractive style than the severe style in which she'd kept her hair before. Her plain, grey gown was stained and ripped in a few places, but she didn't appear to be seriously hurt as he saw only minor bruises. The cat appeared healthy, too, except that one patch of fur on its shoulder was scraped off. Its gold eyes stared at him intently.

"I am glad to see you are alive and well, Mistress Dunncaster." His tone and manner were formal. When she remained silent, he sighed, knowing his task would be all the more difficult.

The cat let out a loud meow, sharp in the morning silence, and the girl stared down at the animal, then she peered up at the general.

"He says you're sincere."

"I am."

"Very well. You are happy—no—glad to see me alive." She had no expression on her face or in her voice, yet he sensed the hurt beneath the surface.

"Yes, and your absence burdens the heart of my emperor. He has looked for you each day we have been here."

"I've watched." Her eyes narrowed. "How did you find me?"

"You left tracks; I followed them. You've been taking food."

"I was hungry."

"Of course," he hastened to say, "and I'm glad you came to the camp. You are most welcome to return with me, Mistress, if you wish. However, there is one thing I don't understand—how did you come to the camp when we kept guard each night?"

"I sang," she explained simply, "and the guard would fall asleep."

He smiled slightly, beckoned toward her and began his way back to the farmhouse. He checked only once, and saw the girl and the cat following at a distance. His smile broadened.

When he entered the house, he found a dozing Ty-Sun reclining against the bear, his head resting on its furry side. His face was turned to the fire; and because his emperor looked so comfortable and at peace, Soong decided he wouldn't say anything yet in case Blessing should bolt out the door, so he sat down. He glanced at Martin, who had seen the girl and the cat and held up one finger to his lips.

Martin nodded, a grin on his face.

Ch'u pranced over to the girl, who stooped to pet him gently.

Ty-Sun drifted in and out of sleep. In his dreams he was home in the Willow Garden again, and Spring Rain was with him and so was Blessing, and he loved both women, but in very different ways, and Martin had become Spring Rain's husband, and she was even now expecting a child as was his own beloved empress. Ch'u had grown fatter than ever, and the bear was completely recovered now, and Ty-Sun's concubines spoiled the beast with candied almonds and honeycakes and stroked the animal until it could have purred had it been a cat.

A shadow fell across him and startled from the pleasantness of his dreams, he fled sleep and opened his eyes.

This was another dream, he told himself, a dream like the other . . . no, a nightmare, then, when he remembered what had happened.

Slowly he rose, not believing what he saw in front of him.

Blessing.

Surely she couldn't be . . . but she was. She was alive. He held out his hands to her.

6

"You murderer!" Blessing cried as she launched herself at Ty-Sun.

Startled, he took a step back, but she would have harmed him had not Martin grabbed her and pulled her away. She struggled against the boy but didn't hurt him as he tried to quiet her. Finally, Blessing indicated that she'd calmed, and somewhat reluctantly Martin released her.

"You have a grievance with the emperor, Mistress Dunncaster?" Soong asked.

"Yes," she said coldly. She glared at Ty-Sun. "You killed my brother." At her feet the cat arched its back and hissed. "My favorite brother, Edmund."

"No, I did not kill your brother," Ty-Sun said, even though he wasn't sure of that. There had been so many men rushing him that night, so many foes to fight. How could he tell which was her brother; yet he had no choice. They both had to know for peace of mind. "I will prove it to you."

He picked up the Orb of White Jade and set it spinning. An amazed expression on her face, she stepped forward and stared down into the milky depths of the Orb. She reached out with one hand, then let it drop slowly to her side.

"What do you see?" Ty-Sun asked gently.

"It's our house, and there are my brothers and my

father . . . and there is Edmund. He has a bandage on one arm but he is able to use it." Her eyes wide, she gazed up at Ty-Sun, and her tone softened. "He's not dead after all."

"No."

Ty-Sun stared into the Orb and saw Miles Dunncaster and knew he had killed the man the night of the ball. He hadn't wanted to harm him, but the man had kept attacking him, and Ty-Sun remembered all too clearly Dragon's Tongue thrusting into his opponent's body. How then that the old man still lived? Sure there was magic in this. He raised his eyes, locked gazes with Soong, who merely stroked his moustache.

The Orb stopped spinning and grew cold once more in his hands. Carefully he slipped it back into a pocket and stood, waiting.

"I'm sorry for falsely accusing you," she said softly, her gaze averted.

"It was understandable." He realized Martin and Soong had slipped from the room allowing them to be alone, and he nearly grinned. "I want to marry you, Blessing." He did not know how else to phrase it. "I wish you to become my empress."

She remained silent, and he grew worried.

"When we met first in the royal garden, and then later when we would talk for hours and hours—didn't you enjoy my company?"

"Yes."

"Then what is amiss, my dear?"

Still she would not look at him. "I think I should return at once to my home and family. They will need me now."

Ty-Sun chuckled as he gently led her to the door. "You are most welcome to go home, if you can, Mistress. As you've doubtless noticed, we are shipwrecked in some unknown land and have no way of going anywhere. So leave, if you so desire, but recall that a woman travelling alone is easy prey to brigands."

"You're threatening me."

"No," he said sadly, "I am only warning you of the dangers which you would face by yourself, Mistress. Some safety lies in numbers, and while our company is not large, it will prove more secure than if we should break up and travel by ourselves. There is always the chance we may help you find your way home. I, too, wish to return home—my land faces destruction, and the longer I delay, the more damage is done."

She did not speak, but this time she looked at him, her eyes compassionate.

"Please, stay with us, Blessing." His eyes, as well as his voice, spoke his desire.

"Very well," she said after a moment's silence, "at least for a while."

"For a while," he agreed.

They left the farmhouse the next day just after dawn. Soong had decided they could no longer linger; he did not think they would find the priest alive or dead now, and so they must move on.

Each member of the small party carried something, and even the bear was laden with supplies. It would do, Soong said, until they could purchase horses or mules in some distant town. Or steal them, he thought to himself, but kept that alternative silent. He also counseled them to stay away from any dwellings until it could be determined whether the inhabitants were hostile or friendly. He did not want them to be too conspicuous, although as he stared at the bear he wondered if that might not prove an impossible task.

They passed through the marshy land, past small houses and buildings. Sometimes they followed along the canals

and waterways crisscrossing the land, but always they
headed eastward. General Soong led, Martin coming behind
with Ty-Sun, then Blessing and the animals bringing up the
rear. Soong was all too aware of the inadequacies of their
small band, but he could do nothing until either they found
men for hire or some mode of faster transportation.

Occasionally as Ty-Sun stretched he saw a flock of black
birds wheeling overhead in the sky, and he knew the Enemy
had sent its spies against him.

He smiled grimly.

They walked until too tired to go any farther, then made
camp and collapsed into bed and sound sleep. The next
morning they were up early and heading eastward again.
Now the land rose gradually, and from time to time they
entered sparse forests. Mostly, though, they passed through
meadows and open countryside. Toward the north they saw
orchards and farms with fields of wheat and oats.

When they camped that night in some woods, scarcely
more than a few oaks and birches and shrubs, Martin and
Blessing volunteered to scout for food as Soong nodded, too
tired to argue. Ch'u plopped down in front of Ty-Sun, who
was sitting with his eyes closed, while the cat slipped off to
prowl in the underbrush.

Blessing found some wild mushrooms while Martin made
a quick visit to one of the orchards and brought back some
fresh fruit. Then he killed several game birds, which they
roasted. No one spoke while they ate, and afterward the
animals promptly curled up in front of the fire and fell
asleep.

"Would you care to accompany me?" Ty-Sun asked
Blessing. Some light still lingered in the sky, and he knew
they would return well before dark.

"All right."

As Ty-Sun strolled beside her, he wanted nothing more
than to clasp her passionately to him, but he knew this

wasn't the time. He would wait; he would be patient. He had decided he would set out to woo her as he had done in England.

She appeared much more rested now, and perhaps knowing her brother still lived had aided. He thanked the gods that Edmund was well, but he still puzzled about the mystery of her father.

They paused when a movement ahead caught their attention, and then both relaxed as the doe, with fawn at her side, darted through the trees.

Neither had spoken since they left the camp, and he knew he must say something. But what?

He stared at the beech trees and elms, then said, "In my country it is the time of renewal."

Her interest piqued, she glanced at him, still without speaking.

"Soon all of my subjects will celebrate the Festival of the Lanterns—a beautiful sight with golden and silver paper lanterns twining in branches and along the sails of the boats. Then shortly afterward comes the rats' wedding night."

"What?" she asked, astounded. Her deep blue eyes gazed at him.

With a pang he thought once more how beautiful she was. Before they had left the farmhouse, she had managed to comb her titian hair with her fingers and had braided it so it no longer floated cloud-like about her. Her cheekbones were set high in an oval face, and she had a long, delicate nose, and a slightly pointed chin. Her mouth was small with pink lips, her arched brows more a soft shade of brown, and her voice was music that caused a thrill to pass through him each time she spoke.

She had mended the tears in her gown and had washed the wide, white collar and apron that had somehow managed to stay on her, although it was much the worse for having been ripped in several places. Her shoes were sturdy and of black leather, and for that at least he did not have to worry.

How he disliked seeing her in such severe plummage. The plain greys and white did not suit her delicate coloring. When they returned to the Land of Ten Thousand Willows, he would dress her in exotic robes. Silks the color of newly plucked peaches, gold and lavender, and the rose and ivory of early mornings. Gowns with delicate embroidery of pheasants and unicorns, and yet as lovely as the clothing might be, it would never be as beautiful as she.

His throat tightened as he considered the sparkling jewels he would bestow upon her, although none as lovely as she, and he wanted to tell her she was a most beautiful woman. But he did not, because he knew it might frighten her. He must go slowly, even though it was agonizing for him.

"What?" she repeated.

He tried remembering what he'd been saying. Ah yes, now he recalled.

"On that night, all members of the household retire early, because it is the night of the rats' weddings, and they come out to celebrate until dawn. When the first rays of sun strike the floor, the rats must then return to their holes."

She laughed, the sound light. "They don't do that. Do they?"

"Of course, they do. I have seen it," he responded gravely.

"You were supposed to retire early!"

"I am the Emperor, after all, and had to know for myself this was a true thing. And it is. They decorate the house with seeds and berries they have saved through the year and then strung together, and they dance for hours."

She still smiled, and he forced himself to keep from reaching out and stroking her cheek. Not yet, not yet, he counseled himself.

He noticed she carried a small bag fashioned out of some cast-off cloth.

"Why did you bring that?"

"Herbs. If possible, I would like to collect a few while we're out this evening. In the days to come they might help us. I can always use them as medicines or to flavor our food."

"An excellent idea."

Her gaze dropped to the pathside, and he was completely bewildered that she would be able to spot anything there. The growth was dense, and his hand went involuntarily to Dragon's Tongue hanging at his side. He must not allow himself to grow lulled; he must watch constantly.

"There's one!" She pointed to the left, then knelt before a tall, stout and wooly plant with spikes of yellow flowers.

"What is this?"

"Mullein. In the old days it was regarded as a charm against the demons, and the Romans would dip it in tallow to use as torches as well. However, I've always used the leaves in poultices for swellings and aches." She rummaged through her bag and pulled out a piece of cloth. He recognized part of one of his robes, one which had not made it whole to shore. She unfolded the material then carefully selected several velvety leaves and a few of the pale yellow flowers, then folded the silk again and returned it to the bag.

"You'll have quite a collection there within a few days," he said with a slightly teasing tone.

"I hope to," she responded somewhat cooly as for the first time he considered that not all the herbs she gathered might be beneficial.

He was so intent in watching her he did not see the branches of a small tree sway behind him or the black shape that slipped closer.

7

Soong watched the couple leave the camp, and he marvelled once again at the great changes that had come over Ty-Sun in this past year. Gone was the languid, bored emperor, who would have forced the girl to marry him, and in his place was a lean, intent man, determined to gently woo the English woman. This emperor was much more to his liking. Perhaps in time Ty-Sun would have changed had he never set foot out of the Garden, but Soong considered this journey—as harsh as it was so far—the best thing for the man.

He watched as Martin busied about the camp, setting things up, then gazed thoughtfully into the darkening forest. Days had passed now since the storm, and everything was very quiet. That made Soong suspicious. He was surprised the Enemy hadn't made a move against them yet, but perhaps he was simply waiting, biding his time.

He sighed. So much to consider, so much to think, and he was so tired. All he wanted was to lie down and sleep for many days and nights, but he couldn't. His emperor needed him.

Soong took out his bow and arrows and thoroughly checked them. He suggested to Martin that he gather up any daggers or swords that they might have and keep them in one place. They didn't have much, but it would have to do for the time being.

Ch'u snored by the fire while the bear grumbled to himself. The cat had disappeared again in the bushes, doubtless to hunt her dinner. Martin had finished his work now and was dozing by the animals.

Soong had explained to Ty-Sun that they would go east and eventually come to the Land of Ten Thousand Willows. True, but it would be long and arduous journey, and Soong wondered if any of them would be alive at the end. Perhaps they should make their way to a coast and hire a boat. No, he knew the avenue of water was closed for all times to them.

It must be the Black Jade Road.

Soong's eyelids drooped, then closed, and he dozed, and when he awakened, cold and stiff, he saw the light had nearly fled from the clearing, and still the couple had not returned.

Blessing had collected several other herbs and explained their various uses to Ty-Sun as they strolled. He had just watched her tuck away another herb when he noticed the light rapidly fading from the forest. Moreover, he noticed how quiet it had grown in the past few moments. He no longer heard the chirping of birds overhead or the rustlings of small animals that accompanied the couple on their walk. Silence sighed through the area. He did not like it.

"We must go back," he said. "I don't want to get lost in unfamiliar woods, and I think we've already strayed too far."

"We can find our way back, can't we?" She gave him an alarmed look.

"Yes, I think so." *I hope so* is what he thought, although he would not admit it.

Ty-Sun had been all too wrapped up in watching Blessing and what she was doing and listening to her voice to mark the passage of time. He sighed. He should have known better, but a man in love, he thought wryly, was sometimes a fool.

She gathered·up her herbs and pouch and slipped the bag across one shoulder then waited for him to say something.

Ty-Sun glanced back through the dim forest. Was that the way they had come? He wasn't sure, but they'd best head toward camp, or where they thought it was. Now, because they had lingered so long, they would probably be returning in darkness, and he did not like that at all. Not at all.

"This way, Blessing."

She nodded, as side by side they began retracing their steps.

Ty-Sun paused as something rustled in the underbrush. He squinted but did not see anything. Why had he waited until the light had fled the sky? He was such a fool. They had no choice, though; they must go on. He strode forward, a determined expression on his face. At least he had remembered to strap Dragon's Tongue on. He would have been a poor warrior to have gone off without some sort of protection.

"What is it?" she asked.

"I don't know. Perhaps it's nothing, yet I think someone—or something—is following us." He didn't want to alarm her, but she should know.

Instead of being frightened, Blessing merely drew her eyebrows together and stared fiercely around them. He was astounded at the change. Gone was the soft-spoken woman; in her place he saw the traces of a warrior of a lost race from the island kingdom of Britain. He loved her all the more.

Leaves crackled to one side while a twig snapped behind them. Ty-Sun, his great sword now resting in his hand, whirled around but once again saw nothing. Whatever was following was pacing them, waiting, playing with them. He little doubted that when the right moment came he and Blessing would be rushed from all sides. If only they could reach the outskirts of camp before then . . . yet he knew they were still too distant.

"Quicken your pace," he said in a low tone. She nodded, the action barely perceptible. In some ways she reminded him of Spring Rain, level-headed and brave. They would need both virtues.

He lengthened his stride now, Blessing hurrying to keep up with his long legs, and his eyes swept from left to right.

He thought he saw eyes like dying embers staring from behind some foliage, and once more he recalled the black dog he had seen in the palace garden in England and then again aboard *The Water Dragon* that last night.

More rustlings ahead and what sounded like a gutteral voice. His stomach tightened in response as he waited, but as he passed the spot nothing happened, and he eased his breath out ever so slightly.

What was following them? What sort of creature . . . creatures . . . could it be?

The gods alone knew.

The gods. He almost smiled at the simplicity. He would entreat the gods and goddesses of the Willow Garden. Surely this was as desperate a situation as the others he'd faced; surely this time the gods would not fail to aid him. Surely.

Ty-Sun stopped so abruptly Blessing nearly collided with him, and he raised his arms with the length of Dragon's Tongue gleaming in the last bit of the day's sunlight.

"Come to me, Kuan-ti, god of war, I beseech you. Hear my words, Erh-lang. Come with the Celestial Dog, and aid me in my time of need. Bring with you Chung K'uei, the great spiritual chaser of demons."

His words rang loudly and defiantly through the silent woods, and he waited. They would hear his words. They would come.

"Erh-lang, Kuan-ti," he called minutes later when no god had appeared, "come aid your friend, Ty-Sun, the One-True and August Emperor of the Land of Ten Thousand Willows."

Seconds passed, and the light on the sword glimmered once then faded. Slowly he lowered Dragon's Tongue. As in the months past, the gods had not responded. It made no difference, Ty-Sun thought with great sorrow, that his own magic had grown significantly since he'd left the Willow Garden so many months before. What mattered was he had failed . . . again.

A low laugh echoed from the couple's right, then with eerie oscillating cries, those who had followed leaped up from their hiding places and surged toward Blessing and Ty-Sun.

8

The creatures facing Ty-Sun and Blessing resembled nothing more than immense piles of putrefying leaves and broken twigs and sloughed-off bark crudely fashioned into a mockery of men. Dark and empty hollows in what might have been faces suggested eyes and mouths. They brought with them the sweet-sour odor of decaying matter that had lain too long on the forest floor.

The first rot-creature, a shambling thing with the partially decomposed body of some unidentifiable small animal woven into its side, threw itself at Ty-Sun. Its long arms ended in hooked claws the color of bleached bones. It snarled, spitting a green-brown drool, and Ty-Sun stumbled backward then gripped his sword more securely. Dragon's Tongue flashed once, slicing wetly through the creature's thick neck.

The square head flew off. The ill-formed hands, black with corruption, groped blindly for the head, but when it couldn't find it, it dropped to the ground and crawled toward Ty-Sun. Horrified, he brought the sword down again and again, hacking and slashing until nothing remained but small pieces.

The head bounced to a stop in front of Blessing, and she backed away then whirled around as something damp pawed her arm. Another creature grinned at her, the putrid skin of its face cracking; a beetle crawled out of its mouth.

It advanced toward her, clicking its claws. She stooped, grabbed a large stick, then, hefting the wood, she clouted the creature. The head snapped back, and it squealed in pain as a chunk of its liquifying face dropped off. It stumbled away, but another creature took its place.

She retreated slowly to a small clearing until she bumped into something. She whirled around, her stick held high, then saw Ty-Sun.

"As soon as I kill one, if you can call it that, it's replaced."

"They aren't going away," she said.

"No, they're not."

Their assailants now numbered nearly fifteen and shuffled as they circled the couple. The only sound was the rustling of the mottled leaves and the clicking claws. Now that he was so close, Ty-Sun could see the bloated black flies swarming around the decay. Obscenely white insects he recognized as maggots burrowed inside the bodies of the creatures.

"It's almost as if they're waiting for something," he mused.

Something rustled in the underbrush beyond them, and he wondered what new horror would come leaping out into the clearing.

Suddenly a black dog appeared, a huge hound with eyes like dying embers. It bared its fangs in savage mockery. The dog he had seen in the palace garden; the dog aboard the ship.

"Where did that come from?" Blessing asked. She edged closer.

"I don't know, but I saw a similar one, or rather this dog, at the palace. And aboard *The Water Dragon* as I fell overboard."

"I don't understand. How could it have followed us so far?"

"It has the help of the Enemy."

The dog growled, the sound rumbling low in its throat, and one of the rot-creatures bent toward the dog, as if listening to the animal's commands.

"This makes things more difficult." Ty-Sun watched the dog. So far the beast hadn't made a move against them which was good. Yet he didn't trust it and knew it would soon attack.

"How so?"

"Before it showed up, I had thought we would charge the creatures, but now . . . now I must think of something to do."

With the back of her hand, Blessing pushed back a stray strand of hair then took a deep breath. "You watch the dog, Your Majesty, and I'll try to take care of the others."

Before the surprised man could ask what she meant, one of the creatures lunged toward them.

The hooked claws swiped at him, ripping one sleeve of his robe and laying his arm bare. Ty-Sun cursed and thrust his sword at the creature, but it danced aside before the metal could do any harm. Out of a corner of his eye, he saw Blessing had drawn away from him, and that she was singing, her voice lilting with that curious and unknown language.

Now why was she doing that? he wondered, then he charged first one attacker, then another. He would try to keep them away from her the best he could. He slashed off arms and heads and claws, and still they kept coming toward him. The sword wasn't killing them; it simply cut them and no more. He didn't have time to hack each one into tiny bits.

The dog threw back its massive head and howled, a

drawn-out sound that chilled him. Then it drew back its pebbly lips, and he saw the white foam flecking the teeth. It bayed again, and he knew the dog planned to kill him, as savagely as it could manage. The animal launched itself at him.

The heavy body hurtled into him before he could raise the sword, knocking him to the ground, and then they were rolling over and over together, the animal's teeth locked fiercely onto his wrist. His sword arm lay beneath him, and as Ty-Sun struggled to free it, the dog ground its teeth against the bones in his wrist. Burning pain coursed through him, and he bit back a scream.

He saw the other creatures closing in on Blessing, and he knew he must do something. He jerked his arm, trying to free his wrist, but the dog's jaws only clamped down harder.

Suddenly the dog released him and howled in pain this time, not triumph.

Puzzled, Ty-Sun scrambled to his feet and watched as the dog whirled around and around, its teeth snapping as it twisted its head left and right trying to seize the small thing clinging to its back.

With the element of surprise, the black and white cat had padded silently into the clearing and leaped upon the dog. Now the feline, all of its razor-sharp claws employed to keep it from falling off, fiercely gnawed the nape of its victim's neck and tender ears. Once more the hound yowled and cast itself upon the ground, desperately attempting to dislodge its tormentor. The cat's claws only sank in deeper, and the dog screamed, droplets of blood flying from its thick coat.

The creatures raised their voices in a combined cry, and half a dozen surrounded Ty-Sun and pressed closer. He gagged as their rotting odor permeated his skin and clothes.

He retched, then plunged Dragon's Tongue into one creature and jerked it out as a brown, watery substance squirted from the body, then whirled lightly around and drove the sword through another.

Minute after minute he cut at them, aware now that bits of their bodies clung to him, and he brushed aside the clammy residue. Once something pale wiggled across a finger, and, repelled, he brushed it against the flat of his sword.

Another attacker swept close, and Ty-Sun's hand brushed against the leaves. Instantly he snatched it away and bit back a cry of pain and glanced down at his skin, now red and puckered, as if some acid had burned it. He rubbed his painful hand against the cool silk of his robe then pierced the creature.

In the past minutes, he'd forgotten Blessing, and now he looked her way to see how she fared. With her back against a tree, she faced several creatures. Yet he saw she was unafraid, and he saw something else that made him pause in astonishment. A handful of what looked like salamanders, no larger than the breadth of a man's hand wavered before her on the ground.

At first he thought the salamanders were attacking Blessing, then he saw she directed them. Scarlet and orange and yellow, the salamanders wavered like gently fanned flames, and with amazement Ty-Sun realized they were composed entirely of fire. As they stepped away from her, they enlarged quickly, soon matching the rot-creatures in size.

A salamander leapt toward a rot-creature and embraced it, and it shrieked as its trunk caught fire. Moldy leaves and maggots sizzled in the flames, and it fluttered to the ground, nothing left beyond ashes.

A second burst into flames, then a third. All those around

her burned now, and without a change in her expression, Blessing stepped forward and sang again. More fire salamanders sprang up from the ground and leaped onto the rot-creatures nearest Ty-Sun. The leaves burned merrily, and the brown fluid he had seen before oozed from the dying things.

The dog yipped piteously and bolted from the clearing. The cat leaped down from its back, and they watched as the dog fled, crashing through the undergrowth. It never looked back.

"Ah, good puss. Your help was most welcome," Blessing said as she stooped to pick up the animal in her arms. She stroked its head and it responded, purring softly. Blood specked the long whiskers.

Ty-Sun took a deep breath and for the first time realized how tired he was. Blessing wore a smudge of ash on one cheek, and he brushed it away.

"Thank you for your assistance."

She nodded, and with the cat still cradled in her arms, she left the clearing. Ty-Sun followed. He wanted to say more, but found himself tongue-tied. Now, too, he was aware of a burning in his hand, but refused to acknowledge the aching. Now he needed to see that they reached the safety of camp first. When he glanced back later, he no longer saw the rot-creatures, and all of the salamanders had disappeared.

They found they weren't far from camp, and when they entered it, complete darkness having fallen, Martin and Soong rushed toward them.

"Are you all right, my lord, my lady?" Martin asked, his eyes wild. "I was worried sick. The general here was worried, too. When you didn't come back hours ago, we suspected something had happened and were about to set out when—"

"Yes, yes, calm down, my boy," Soong said soothingly, clapping a hand on Martin's shoulder, "they're obviously fine." He peered closely at them in the flickering light of the fire. "Although it's apparent they've had an encounter. Come sit down and have something to eat, then tell us what detained you."

Ty-Sun and Blessing did as bid, and as they ate, they took turns recounting the attack. Martin shuddered, while Soong simply nodded, thoughtfully stroking the good side of his moustache.

Martin rewarded the cat with a firm pat and a full dish for playing such an important part in their defense, and when finished eating, it began meticulously grooming its whiskers.

"You say you'd seen this dog before?" Ty-Sun nodded. "Yet you mentioned nothing to me."

"I deemed it unimportant at the time. I see I was sadly mistaken." He praised Blessing for conjuring the fire salamanders, acclaim that brought a blush to her cheeks. "I don't know if we would have survived if it hadn't been for Blessing."

"Nonsense," she replied matter-of-factly.

"No, you were a true warrior today."

Martin offered them more stew that both accepted heartily, having worked up an appetite during the battle, and as Ty-Sun shifted, he winced, and Blessing demanded to know where he hurt.

"I'm not injured," he said shortly.

"You are," she insisted and grabbed his hand. Once more he winced. She studied the puckered wound then set his hand down carefully. "I have something in my bag for that."

She drew out a few mustard-yellow seeds then poured some water onto the ground away from the fire. With a small stick she stirred the water and dirt until thick, then she sprinkled the seeds into it, and, picking up the mud, kneaded it. When it was thoroughly combined, she slathered the poultice on his hand and ripped off the hem of her apron as a bandage.

Ty-Sun could feel the burning subsiding as the medicated mud soothed. Since touching the creature, his hand had grown increasingly numb, but the process was so gradual, he hadn't noticed until he flexed abruptly.

"Thank you," he said again.

She shrugged and went to wash her hands in the nearby stream.

Surprised, Soong looked after the woman then at Ty-Sun, who carefully studied the bandage and prudently said nothing.

✳— 9 —✳

It was Chung Ch'iu, the Harvest and the Festival of the Moon, and the inhabitants of the Willow Garden were celebrating on this fifteenth day of the Eighth Moon, and in the imperial palace and city numerous entertainments were underway.

Ty-Sun lolled upon a comfortable divan covered in bright silks and watched as several of his concubines danced. They were acting out the birth of the moon, and Never Grieve in a flowing robe of silver and gold silk portrayed the lady moon. She rose from the plum-colored cushion upon which she knelt, and her plump arms stretched far above her head as she sang her lines.

He judged her as one of the best actors among his court, and only the previous moon she had enacted the part of the Celestial Weaving Maid, who met her lover once a year on a bridge formed by magpies. At the conclusion of the moving performance, he presented her with a bracelet of jade links.

Scarlet and gold and peach and turquoise paper lanterns burned overhead; a slight breeze swayed them, making the lights dance. In the corners of the great room he glimpsed dark shadows, and sometimes from those depths he saw eyes like dying embers.

However, he was enjoying himself tonight and so turned away and watched the dancers and the singers as Tsu-ying plucked the strings of the *qin*, a zither, in accompaniment. Her narrow-plucked eyebrows were painted green in the style called the Imitation of the Kingfisher, while carmine stained her cheeks and lips. Her richly embroidered robes were white, and he wondered for whom she mourned, and when he regarded her more closely he could see the tears yet unshed in her eyes.

As he gazed at his court members, he saw now they all wore white, and he drew his black eyebrows together in puzzlement. Who was dead? And why had he not been informed? He studied his own robe. He wore one of red with gold dragons embroidered in the front and lions and pheasants along the hem, and yet there were holes in the material as if something sharp had slashed it. What had happened here? Why had he dressed in such a shabby garment?

Curious, he thought, but then his attention returned momentarily to his consort, who one moment wore the face of Spring Rain, in the next that of Blessing Dunncaster. She wore an ornate gown of the western fashion, and even as he watched, droplets of blood seeped through bloodstains on the bodice.

She had just finished eating a round moon cake and was licking the crumbs off her fingers. She laughed then and took a sip of cinnamon wine and spoke to him, but he couldn't understand her words. So he nodded politely as he accepted a jade and coral goblet of iced wine from a servant who bowed and backed away.

Beyond, on an immense table, sat the refreshments. Watermelons cut in the lotus shape, spiced figs and peaches, sesame seed balls with a sweet plum filling, fresh persimmons, grapes and loquats, honeyed bamboo shoots, sugared almonds, pine seeds and pistachios, candied dates, as well as roast duck in spices and striped mullet. Cinnamon and chrysanthemum wine in which tiny orchids floated, and a rice beer that proved so strong he could only take an occasional sip provided some of the liquid refreshment. Flies droned above the food, while something small and white wiggled across the tablecloth, disappearing behind the figs. He frowned, but couldn't see anything now.

The gods and goddesses had come to the Moon Festival, too, and he recognized Sao Ch'ing Niang, the Goddess of Fine Weather, chatting with Lei Kung, the Thunder God, and Yu Nu, the Jade Maiden. Beyond them sat, arguing as always, the Eight Immortals, with the one woman in the midst of the seven men. To his left sat Erh-lang, the Celestial Dog lolling at his feet, and Sheng-mu. A good-natured group had gathered in celebration of the female principle of the moon, and he was pleased all his friends had managed to attend.

Erh-lang introduced three new arrivals, whom Ty-Sun saw were fire salamanders dressed in the elaborate satins and velvets of King Charles' English court. As he stared at the flames, he puzzled why the cloth did not catch on fire. Magic, he marvelled, and blinked as the salamanders bowed low. He greeted each one by name, even though he wasn't sure he'd caught their names, and they said they came with urgent news. He reminded them they were here to enjoy themselves and beckoned, the long silver nail-guards clicking, to servants to bring these new guests food and wine.

Hands clasped behind his back in precisely the manner of his old tutor, Ty-Sun began lecturing the fire salamanders on the yin-yang, which maintained that everything within the universe was divided between two principles: masculine and feminine, sun and moon, heaven and earth, fire and water, light and dark, summer and winter, life and death, east and west. And these forces, he said, remained eternally in opposition. Sometimes the yang, or masculine, was more powerful, sometimes the yin, or feminine, grew dominant.

They mustn't be very interested, he thought ruefully, because they weren't paying strict attention to him. Perhaps he was not a good lecturer. He decided he would detail this concept for them.

However, Ch'u appeared then and was talking, and he was surprised he could understand the little dog. A black and white cat sat behind the dog and licked one bloody paw, and Ty-Sun wondered if she had caught a mouse. Perhaps that was what he had seen on the refreshment table. He shuddered at the memory.

The salamanders were clamoring for his attention now, and a somewhat tipsy Lei Kung demanded these ill-mannered foreigners be thrown out of the festival immediately. The Eight Immortals nodded, in agreement for once.

Ch'u defended the salamanders now, saying they came with an urgent message, and as Ty-Sun stared, bemused, at the dog, he caught a flicker of motion from the corner of his eye.

He turned his head quickly and saw someone, a stranger, standing just inside the door, and Ty-Sun suspected he should know who this person was. After all, he didn't invite those whom he did not know well to the festival. But the person was swathed from head to foot in black, and so he could not see the face.

The room darkened, the fires flickered out, and the floor trembled while a great rumble filled the air, and at that moment, the flies lit upon the food, and maggots, white and loathsome, crawled through the fruit and nuts. His consort screamed, and he watched in horror as her flesh sloughed from her face, leaving only bone. Never Grieve collapsed upon the floor, and Ch'u tore at her flesh. The cat leaped upon an actor, scratched his face, drawing tiny streams of blood. The salamanders brushed against the pillows and silks and curtains, and the material burst into flames.

Ty-Sun screamed and, standing, raised one hand and commanded that the stranger go. Around him concubines and actors shrieked, and from somewhere in the room a dog howled.

The dark figure laughed, and in that moment Ty-Sun knew who it was.

The Enemy.

"The Enemy, the Enemy," Ty-Sun murmured as he tossed on his bed of fire. His skin, his blood, his mind, everything around him and in him was on fire, and he burned. He could have been one of the salamanders called forth by Blessing, and when he spread his fingers, flames shot forth from their tips.

Once more he saw the face of his consort, the concubines, and court members. Worms and maggots crawled into their ears and out of their mouths, leaving a trail of glistening slime behind them, and smelling the stench of their deaths, he gagged.

He saw the rot-creatures, and above, the firebirds that he and his friends had fought after leaving Russland. A great wind rose and fanned the flames of his body and the firebirds until the ships, the people, the land, everything around him burned. All the while he smelled the fetidness of the rotting creatures as they breathed upon him.

As Ty-Sun watched sadly, his beloved ones decayed and mouldered and finally collapsed into piles of grey dust that blew away in the wind, and he heard the Enemy's taunting laugh and the whisper that he, too, would soon be dead.

He tried to call out, but couldn't speak. He could only burn and burn and burn.

Then something cold and moist swept across his forehead and cheeks, down his body, and the fire dimmed a little. He struggled to open his eyes, yet was unable, and still the coolness caressed him.

Gradually the flames died down until they were no more than embers, and then he could open his eyes effortlessly. Above him he saw Blessing, a worried expression on her face.

"Wh-what's wrong?" he asked, his voice trembling slightly. He was cold, so very cold now; the fire which had waged so long within him had flickered out completely. Chilling shudders racked him, one after the other, while the ice seeped down into his bones. Had winter come already?

"You had a fever for several days, Ty-Sun," she said, her voice soft. "I thought I'd drawn all the poison from you with the poultice, but apparently enough remained to make you quite ill." Again the wet coolness caressed his forehead, his cheeks, his neck. A cloth he saw; she was bathing his hot skin.

"A fever," he repeated, feeling as if he were no more than a child. "Days?" She nodded. He was bewildered. Everything he'd experienced in what he now knew was a fever-induced dream had been so real that he felt he should say something to Blessing, warn her perhaps of the danger. He saw Soong's face beyond her shoulder and Martin's, too, and the young man looked as if he were on the verge of tears. Ty-Sun tried to tell the boy everything was all right, that he would be fine, even though he wasn't sure about that, but no words came.

Martin's face spun away, and Soong's hung upside down, and Blessing's blue eyes were melting, and he thought he saw the bear gazing sadly at him. Beyond the beast stood a silent shadow. Ty-Sun's eyes rolled up as he slid into an uneasy sleep.

Two mornings later Ty-Sun's fever fell and then by midafternoon was finally gone, and he rested easily after that. While the emperor slept soundly, Soong asked Blessing when she supposed he might be well enough to travel.

"In a day or two at the very soonest, General," she replied slowly, "but it would be much better if he rested longer."

Soong sighed as he stared at the sleeping man. His thin face was pale, and Soong remembered the days and nights when he and Martin had taken turns with Blessing watching over him. His skin had glowed then as if he burned from the inside out, and the general was surprised he had survived.

"I fear we can't linger any longer, and yet we have no choice. We'll leave when you say it's time, Mistress Blessing."

That evening Martin brought Ty-Sun his meal and he ate slowly, savoring the broth. It was the first time he had eaten in nearly a week. That night he slept without any dreams, and in the morning he felt completely refreshed and recovered from his illness.

He dressed in the one fresh robe left to him, slipped the amber beads around his neck—they must be working as an amulet, he thought wryly; after all, he was still alive—then sat down beside Soong on a flat rock.

"You're looking much better today." Soong's gruffness belied the concern he had felt while the emperor had tossed in his fevered sleep.

"I feel fine, General." Ty-Sun gazed at the puckered wound on his hand. Only faintly red now, it no longer burned, and as he brushed his fingertips across it, he marvelled at the wondrous healing skill in Blessing's hands.

"Fine enough to travel?"

"Yes."

"Good. We've stayed here far too long, but we had no choice in the matter. Some of those rot-creatures might still linger in the area."

Ty-Sun shook his head. "No, I think the dog somehow called them forth, just as Blessing did with the fire salamanders."

"Perhaps, but I wouldn't want to wager money on that." Soong sighed, spit in his hand, and rubbed the dust from his boots. "The gods alone know what the Enemy will send our way next."

"Yes," Ty-Sun said grimly, "the gods alone know." And as he well knew, the gods no longer seemed on a speaking basis with him.

❧— *10* —❧

Farther east the land changed. The four companions left the plain along the coast and passed into a higher elevation, and what had started as low foothills sloped upward into full-grown mountain ranges. The forest grew denser, too, with tall pines and beech and oaks now prevalent. Here, too, in the damper soil they found spruce, balsam and silver firs.

Blessing pointed out those flowers she recognized. The strange, white, hood-shaped flowers with the fingerlike leaves she identified as monkshood, sometimes called wolfsbane, which was exceedingly poisonous, so they must never handle them, she warned. Yet the bell-shaped flowers clustered on tall stalks, delicately shaded purple or yellow or white were known as foxglove and could be used medicinally.

She paused, picking a few of the latter for her herb pouch. She said the little purple flowers amidst the dark green leaves were violets and could be used for scents; she did not stop for them, although Ty-Sun found them quite charming.

Profuse wildlife roamed freely, and nearly each day they spotted woodpeckers and beavers and red deer. At night they listened to the hooting of owls and the distant screams of wildcats.

During the day Martin and Soong stopped and fished in the cold mountain streams, and at night they ate the fish they caught along with any berries, plentiful in these forest, that they might have picked earlier. Sometimes Soong or Martin brought down a wild boar, and when they did, they smoked the meat and packed it so they could eat it when game was scarcer.

In the past few days the journey had grown almost idyllic for Ty-Sun. Even though they covered as much distance as they could each day, and even though his legs nearly always ached, he enjoyed his time spent with Blessing for they chatted much as they walked and at night around the campfire.

Watching her, Ty-Sun found he could almost forget they were not on a leisurely jaunt and did not have all the time in the world to return to the Willow Garden; he could almost forget the Enemy. Almost.

Soong agreed with Ty-Sun it was a remarkable land, but inside he remained uneasy. Too many trees stood too closely together, and at times the sun could scarcely be glimpsed through the thick twining of branches overhead. The day ended too quickly for the light disappeared from the forest long before the sun had set. Sometimes the birds fell unnaturally silent, and it was then he was most disturbed.

From time to time the old general looked back to see if they were being followed but saw no one. Of course, that didn't mean they were alone; still, he kept alert, reminded them to keep their swords or daggers by their sides—day or night—and waited for something to happen. He knew it was just a matter of time.

Some days past Soong had found a scrap of bark and decided to use it for counting the days. With the tip of a dagger he scratched a mark for each day that elapsed. He knew how long they'd been away when they sailed from England, but it was the time from their shipwreck that he wanted to record. It would be all too easy to lose track of the days which could prove a fatal mistake.

Ty-Sun eased his scuffed boots off, letting them drop onto the ground and glared at his reddened feet. He sat down abruptly and eased them into the stream. Coolness assailed his overheated, overtired feet, and he breathed more easily.

Soong watched with amusement as he dropped his bow and arrowcase onto the ground. "You would never have made a foot soldier, my friend."

"Perhaps," Ty-Sun said, lifting an eyebrow, "but not even your most elite soldiers marched this far in a single day, Soong."

The general smiled. "Now, you know that's not so, Your Majesty. Sometimes they would go twice as far as we did today."

"Please." Ty-Sun closed his eyes and lay back on the bank.

Soong leaned over the stream and, cupping his hands, splashed water onto his face and neck. The water was icy and refreshing, and he drank long. Then he leaned back, resting on his elbows and stared across the sun-dappled water.

The next morning the small group rose well before dawn to eat a cold breakfast, then broke camp and began marching. Soong urged them to walk even faster than usual, but reminded them to keep their eyes open for edible berries and for game. Although summer had just started, he said autumn would be upon them before long and then winter, and they must have food for those seasons. Yet they could hardly be expected to cart all that upon their backs.

The four companions camped that afternoon along the

stream's bank on high ground in case of flooding, and here the trees dropped away slightly revealing a small meadow. Here, too, they could see the sun, still high in the sky, and even though early, Soong had decided they could stop for the day. Martin was setting up the camp, while Blessing washed her face and hands then set about examining the flowers in the meadow.

"We need horses or donkeys," Ty-Sun said, his eyes still closed. He mustn't sleep now; there was dinner yet, and he and Soong had to talk. He shook his head to wake himself up.

"I know. We are already overloaded and are losing distance every day."

"There are the animals, too. I know they slow us down, but we cannot turn them loose. I would never forgive myself. Besides, the cat saved us from the black dog. Who knows what will come?"

"True."

"Where will we find the beasts? You don't want us to go into a town."

"We'll have to, I think. Still, I would like us to be beyond these woods, if we ever do find the end, that is."

Ty-Sun yawned again.

"Am I keeping you awake?"

He heard the irony in Soong's voice and straightened. "No, no, not at all. I mean, I wasn't about to fall asleep."

"You look like that cat of Blessing's right now with your face up to the sun."

He mustered as much dignity as he could for his reply. "We haven't seen the sun in a while, and I plan on enjoying it."

Silence fell between them for a while. Ty-Sun's feet were feeling much better now; they were definitely cooler, and he thought they wouldn't hurt much that night. Some evenings his sore feet had keep him awake. He opened one eye and glanced at Soong. The general's eyes were closed, and Ty-Sun assumed his friend was asleep. Good, then he could rest now. He sighed deeply, feeling comfortable for the first time that day. He yawned and settled back to doze.

"The Black Jade Road."

"What?" Ty-Sun looked at Soong, saw the general was all too wide awake.

"The Black Jade Road," Soong repeated. "Do you know what that is, Your Majesty?"

"A road made of black jade?"

A disgusted sound came from Soong. "Yes, but it is more than that. Did your father never tell you about the road?"

"My father revealed little of the mysteries of my exalted position, Soong. His death was far too unexpected for him to plan any such thing; he presumed he would live many more years."

"Hmmmm." Once more Soong lapsed into a tactful silence.

When minutes passed and his friend didn't speak, Ty-Sun stirred impatiently. "Well, aren't you going to tell me?"

"Yes, yes." Soong stroked his moustache and stared into the sparkling water. "Once, long ago, the Land of Ten Thousand Willows was much larger. That is, its empire stretched far beyond the current borders. The emperor and empress of the time were extremely interested in the outside world, and they dispatched numerous diplomats and ambassadors into distant lands. After a time, treaties were finally signed, and so that the messengers and merchants and other travellers might go quickly throughout the empire, the Black Jade Road was laid. It is indeed, as you surmised, Your Majesty, a road of black jade, smooth and wide, and yet it is more than that. It is a magic road, too."

"Magic?"

"Yes. The traveller upon it seems to walk or ride at the same rate as always, and yet the distance passes quickly. So a journey which would normally take thirty days is finished in half the time."

"Ah. Does this road still exist?"

"I believe it does, although it has not been used by any from the Garden for many years. Before your father's time, the Willow Garden acquired its current borders, and general knowledge of the road passed from the lives of those dwelling in the Garden. Only the emperor or empress remembered it, as well as those few to whom they divulged this secret." Soong squinted at Ty-Sun. "Only a member of the imperial family can see the road, you see; it remains invisible to all others. I want us to try to find that road and travel along it because it will cut down on our travelling time considerably."

"I understand. An excellent suggestion, as always, Soong. But where is it? How far west did it come? How shall we find it?"

Soong shook his head slightly. "I know the road stretched through most of Russland, and as for beyond that, I don't know. If I remember my maps correctly, we need to go east some distance more, then head north. Then we should encounter it."

"Russland. Hmm. We were not well received when we visited there."

"True, but we are not returning to the court of Tsar Mikhail. At least, I don't intend to!"

"Neither do I. Good, good. We will go to this Black Jade Road. I like that name."

"Umm, yes."

"There's something else, Soong?"

"Yes, Your Majesty."

Ty-Sun raised an eyebrow ever so slightly. "What is it

then?" He tried ignoring the small protest from deep within himself. One part of him did not want to hear Soong's next words.

"While the road is fast, it is also dangerous. It goes through some of the worst terrain, past some of the most murderous tribes. In other words, we will not have an easy time of it."

Ty-Sun sighed. "Frankly, I'm not surprised. But then we have no choice, do we?"

"No, Your Majesty, we don't."

"Then it's the Black Jade Road for us." And may the gods finally help us, he added silently.

The man in black paused behind the thicket. From a distance he could hear voices floating on the wind. He listened intently: a woman and several men and some animals. It was those he sought.

He smiled, but the expression faded as the pain in his face and his back swept through him again. Blood dripped in small droplets from his injured arm, and he pressed his fingertips lightly against the wound. Ever since the cat had jumped onto him when he was in the other form, he had hurt. But he had no time to pause to tend to his wounds. The One waited.

He crept silently through the woods, skirting the camp along the stream, and watched as the young man and woman prepared a meal, watched as the tall man and the old general returned from the river.

He watched, then slipped through the woods, going deep into them. Here the sun did not penetrate to the forest's floor, and darkness reigned. Trees, old and diseased, stretched far above his head. Branches, weighed down with mold, drooped almost to the ground. Occasionally he heard the rustle of some animal or saw the glint of a creature's eyes. Well, he wasn't worried; nothing would attack him here.

He arrived at the spot long before the sun set, but here it was already as dark as midnight on a moonless night. Yet he could see as perfectly as if it were daytime.

He smiled at the image of carved stone setting at the base of a mammoth tree then knelt before it. He clasped his hands together, then prayed silently a long time to the One. With his unscathed hand, he rubbed the image's cheek, then kissed the stone lips and shivered as their coldness seeped into his body, invading the very warmth of his being.

He smeared blood from his wound across the statue, dabbing red on the head, face, body. Beneath his fingers the stone throbbed.

He heard the voice.

You have done well so far, but your wounds must heal so you may be strong, so that you may lead our warriors into battle.

The pain in his body increased until he bit his lips to keep from crying out, then slowly the pain in his back and legs and arms ebbed away. Within a few minutes none of his wounds hurt.

"Truly a miracle," whispered Fray Villadiego as he smiled at the dark visage.

⊱••— *11* —••⊰

In the week since Ty-Sun and his friends had left the
meadow and stream, the terrain had gradually roughened
and the forest thickened, growing so densely now that often
they were forced to go single file. The forest now remained
almost entirely silent, and in the quiet they could hear their
footsteps and the snuffling of the bear as he followed.

No birds chirped in the trees; no small animals prowled in
the bushes, and Soong believed these were ominous signs.
He did not like it at all. It was odd, too, that they had met
no other humans on this journey. Where were the people?

Occasionally they stumbled upon clearings containing
houses, and yet when they paused, still keeping out of sight,
they saw no one stirring. No smoke puffed from the
chimneys, no farm animals stood in the pens. They found
village after village like this, and when they searched
through the houses, they found no clue to the disappearance
of the inhabitants.

The farther east the companions progressed, though, the
more ravaged were the villages. At first the hamlets and
houses had simply been deserted, now they found most
were destroyed, having been burned to the ground. Only
ashes and charred wood and a few scorched stone walls
remained standing. Sometimes they found bodies that had

been left for months or even longer, and quietly and quickly they buried the dead.

They searched those houses intact and found some foods still unspoiled that they took with them. Since they'd seen no small game animals in some time, they'd had no fresh meat. Now Soong grew more worried they might run out of food before reaching the Willow Garden; he kept reminding himself that autumn lay in the not too far distant future.

Sometimes they found the cattle and sheep slaughtered, the meat too spoiled to save.

"Who would do such a thing?" Martin asked.

"The same men who wage the wars," Soong replied quietly.

"Then you think a war has driven the people away?"

"Yes. I can think of no other reason—except perhaps disease, and even then, I think they would have saved some of their belongings. As you've seen for yourself, these people fled without taking anything." Soong pushed aside charred wood with the tip of his boot. "War waged by men for religion's sake, I think."

"Those who started the war can't be very religious," Martin said, hunching his shoulders as he surveyed the ruins.

"No, but they think they are, but all they do is perpetuate half-truths and distrust and hatred. Small comfort to those who lived here once." Soong walked away without looking back.

When they reached another clearing later in the day, Ty-Sun gazed up into the grey sky to see birds circling overhead, the first they had seen in days. The Enemy's spies, he wondered? Could they go nowhere without them? Sighing wearily, he rubbed his face. He was tired and wanted to stop for the night, but not here, not in this dead place. It made him too uneasy.

Since morning they'd heard the distant rumble of thunder and now the rain fell at last. It poured relentlessly, and soon they were drenched to the skin. The bear, its thick fur plastered down, muttered its protest, while the cat distastefully picked its way through the puddles.

Finally they found a shallow cave on high ground, and there they camped. The rain stopped even as Martin searched for dry wood. He found a few branches and twigs in the cave. They huddled around the warmth of the fire and later dined on dried meat and some fruit taken from one of the villages. No one felt much like talking, and quite early, Martin, the dog and cat accompanying him, retired to bed.

Soong and Ty-Sun talked quietly for a while, then the general went to bed. Blessing, sitting away from the fire, gazed at Ty-Sun. The yellow light touched the planes of his face, and she thought him a very handsome man. He looked different from any other man she had ever seen with his tilted eyes and long black hair, but he was regal with a proud and yet compassionate expression. His colorful robe was no longer intact, and even the trousers he wore underneath looked stained and ragged.

Ruefully she considered how she must look. Like a hoyden, no doubt, with straggling hair, an apron ripped apart for bandages, and a gown so torn along one sleeve that her shoulder was barely concealed.

What would her father think?

Her eyes filled with tears. She missed Ned, and she missed home. She did not think she would ever see her home or brother again.

Glancing at Ty-Sun, she saw his eyes were closed. He looked weary, and she suspected he hadn't recovered completely from his fever. He protested he had, but at times she thought his eyes glimmered, as though he were still in the throes of the poison. Yet he never complained of pain or discomfort, for which she admired him. She admired him for other reasons, too, and color darkened her cheeks.

"I have never thanked you," he said, his quiet voice startling her.

"For what?"

"For coming to warn me the night of the ball. It was a brave thing."

"I did not come that night for that. I had sent a message before that."

"What?" Ty-Sun scowled. "How was the message sent, Blessing?"

"I went one night to the palace to warn you—I had overheard my father and Cromwell discussing their plans—but the priest said you were not there presently, and that I could trust him with the message. Did he not give it to you?"

"No." Ty-Sun stared into the flames, then lifted his eyes to her. "The priest relayed no message. I can think of only one thing—that somehow he must have allied himself with your father and the others."

"Their religions are not the same, and my father never tolerated Catholics. Indeed, he hated anyone not of his own faith."

"True, but the influence of the Enemy blurs many distinctions, I think." He shook his head. "No wonder the priest was so eager to journey with me. I had a spy from the Enemy with me the entire time. It's a wonder any of us escaped with our lives." He thought of the black dog. Surely now he must see it was the priest changed into animal form. And he recalled, too, that Spring Rain had always distrusted the priest. With good reason, he knew now.

He closed his eyes again. "There's still so much left, such a long distance, and so much blood stains my hands. General Soong is a wise man and urged I travel lightly. Yet

when we set out on our expedition, I believed it would be a
lark and so I brought my old tutor, my musicians and
tumblers and actors; I included numerous advisors as well
as my favorite concubine; I brought household guards, my
best cooks, and countless useless others. We progressed
leisurely, this immense bloated company, because we could
do nothing else. Little by little the Enemy picked away at
us, killing some in the Great Ice, some at sea, some in
England, and the remainder in the shipwreck. All who came
with me are gone—except General Soong and my faithful
Ch'u."

The dog, hearing his name, raised his head slightly,
blinked in the light of the fire, yawned, then went back to
sleep.

"It wasn't your fault."

"Ah, but it was."

"You couldn't have known what you would be facing.
No man could."

"Kind words to mask what a fool I was. I should have
listened to Soong. He knew; he suspected what would
happen. I was too proud, too stubborn, and listened only to
my selfish whims and desires. And see what grief it has
brought us all to."

"No!"

He opened his eyes and gazed at her. Her blue eyes
blazed.

"I will not countenance self-pity in any man, Ty-Sun, and
least of all in you. There is no reason for it. At the time you
did what you thought best; now you see it wasn't. But not
all is lost. We are yet alive, and we *will* reach the Willow
Garden. We will reach it before the time is up."

Ty-Sun was astounded. No woman had ever spoken to
him thusly, not even Spring Rain. A momentary anger rose
in him, replaced at once by respect.

"Very well, I will listen to your wise words, for I know in my heart—even if my mind will not accept it—that you are right."

"Indeed, I am." She smiled at him.

"You mentioned moments ago the religion of your father, or so you phrased it. Were you not also a Puritan?"

"I was not considered one. As you know, I have always been different from my family. Although raised in my father's faith, I could not believe in a stern and unloving God. Yet my father was determined to mold me into his own strict image. Sometimes when he was angry with me, and that was often, he called me a she-cousin to the Devil and beat me unmercifully, the better to exorcise the demon, or so he claimed. According to family legend, I resembled my long-dead great-grandmother, a red-haired woman burned at the stake as a witch. My red hair branded me the same and my father always believed it proof of a devilish alliance. I was always able to talk with cats and dogs and birds and sing to them, but only my brother Ned knew to what extent I could understand the animals. And yet, I swear I have never made a pact with the Devil. One can be a witch, and not be evil."

"I know that," Ty-Sun said softly. "You could never be evil, my dear."

She did not speak, and he shifted slightly so he sat next to her and slipped an arm about her shoulders. She rested her head upon him, and they stared into the dying fire.

☙— *12* —❧

Several days later Ty-Sun and the others camped along a river running deep within a lush valley. Martin, who had scouted ahead, had spotted a village perched on the mountainside not far away—and all its residents were very much alive. Soong said he didn't know why, but perhaps the war had skipped around this single village, or else it hadn't stretched this far yet.

Soong was encouraged. Now they'd trade some of Ty-Sun's gems for horses, four for riding, one as a pack animal. He guessed Martin would attract the least attention of any of them, so the next day the young man set out to make the transactions. Because his previous employer, Lord Elphinstone, had insisted on having educated servants, Martin had learned several languages in his years of service. When he met the blacksmith, he tried a range of different languages on the bewildered man until finally he made himself understood in German. Martin produced several pearls and one small sapphire and received the animals he wanted.

Soong was waiting just outside the village to help lead the horses back to camp.

"This is going to proceed much slower than I'd anticipated," Soong muttered when they returned to the camp.

"These animals are hardly fit to be called horses, although Martin claims they were the best the man had to offer."

Ty-Sun stared at the horses. Three, with their ribs showing, were obviously old and should have long ago been put out to pasture. The fourth was far younger, but was skittish, shying at every noise, the whites of its eyes showing. The other horse, a heavyset draft horse, would doubtless look much better after a few meals and would carry their supplies.

Soong chose the skittish horse for his as he had the most experience riding, while Ty-Sun claimed the tallest, a roan whose shoulder blades were level with the emperor's. While the horse was far from young, Ty-Sun knew the animal still possessed heart, and as he stood and stroked the horse's muzzle, the roan whickered and blew gently into his face.

At first the horses feared the bear, who cowered when he in turn saw them, but after Blessing stroked the horses and whispered into their ears, they no longer trembled when the bear ambled past.

For the next week they followed the course of the river and took an easy pace, allowing the horses to rest and eat as much grass as they wanted. By the end of seven days, Martin swore he could already see a change in their mounts.

The next night when they camped, Martin and Blessing both fell asleep immediately after dinner, while General Soong took the first watch.

Ty-Sun took the Orb of White Jade from his pocket and gazed at it. The last time he had spun the Orb, he had shown Blessing her brother still lived; the time before that he encountered the Enemy. Or rather, he had encountered the Enemy's devotees. Would he ever see his adversary? What was he like? Was he a man, was he human? Certainly the Enemy was a great sorcerer, one that matched Ty-Sun's own powers, and Ty-Sun wondered how the Enemy had gained his.

He shuddered, then looked away from the white jade. He must do it. He must see into the Enemy's land again. But at what price? Previously he had nearly been captured by the Enemy. No matter the outcome, he knew he must enter the plane again.

He stroked the cold Orb, establishing contact with it, then began spinning it between his palms. As it rotated the Orb grew whiter and warmer, until it glowed with a bright light. His breathing slowed, his eyelids lowered, and he entered the trance.

When he opened his eyes, he was not surprised to see the blackness. Once, long ago, he would have seen an astral plane lit by a silver light, but that was gone. Now the darkness pressed against him, as though seeking to smother him, and this time he was prepared for it. He drew out the astral Dragon's Tongue, sparks flying from the metal, and sliced through the enveloping darkness. Shreds of black clung to the sword as he thrust it into the darkness again and again.

Gradually he saw light through the patches cut in the darkness, and finally the blackness lessened, and he could see. Once more the plane was flat with no distinguishing features, not even the crooked black spire he'd seen last time.

This was neither a bad nor a good place, but one completely neutral. He hadn't known that before his last venture, but his Enemy had and had worked that knowledge to his benefit. Now, Ty-Sun thought, the Enemy must control the plane, and from there . . . it would be one easy step to control the Earth.

As he walked, he felt the cold from the ground seeping through his boots, climbing his legs, numbing his hands. A slight breeze brought with it a fetid odor, reminding him of the rot-creatures he and Blessing had faced, and his grip on the sword tightened.

All he experienced here was as real as if he were awake. He could be injured here; he could be killed; and his other body would die then.

The ground rose gradually, and he ascended into low hills. Beyond lay greyness, and occasionally he used the astral Orb for light. At times he saw shrivelled bushes and vines, stunted trees, and those that looked blasted by lightning. The path he trod was gravelly, and when he stooped to examine the pebbles, he saw they were the bones and skulls of small animals, broken into thousands of pieces. Grimly he rose to his feet.

For some time clouds had roiled overhead, then quickly gathered, dark clouds promising rain and a tumultuous storm. Now as lightning flashed bone-white and thunder muttered ominously, Ty-Sun saw a troop of mysterious horsemen galloping across the sky weaving in and out of the clouds. Their leader wore a flowing mantle the color of midnight and a wide-brimmed hat and was mounted on a white horse.

As Ty-Sun watched, the lead horseman twisted his head and stared down at him, then swerved his mount toward the ground. The other riders charged past and disappeared into the dark clouds, while the lone horseman galloped toward Ty-Sun.

The rider leaped from the horse when it was still a few feet above the ground and tore off his mantle and hat, tossing them aside. The horse snorted and shook its head, and long icicles hanging from its bridle flew loose and shattered as they hit the ground. The horseman had long, flowing hair the color of cornsilk, and his eyes glinted an icy blue. Bits of hair and bone decorated his leather armor.

Without warning, the blond warrior flung himself forward, thrusting his sword at Ty-Sun, who managed with little time to spare to leap aside before he was run through. His opponent's sword caught a piece of Ty-Sun's robe, and where the blade sliced, the cloth burned with a cloying odor. The other smiled thinly, his eyes of ice unreadable.

Thunder rumbled as the two opponents slowly circled each other. Ty-Sun watched this man warily; he wasn't sure what to expect. The warrior advanced again, swinging his sword toward Ty-Sun, who parried, thrusting Dragon's Tongue against the other's weapon. The warrior stumbled backward, recovered, and rushed Ty-Sun. They fought, no sound except for the clanging of sword against sword, and each time the warrior attacked, Ty-Sun managed to leap aside.

Sweat rolled from Ty-Sun's face, yet the other appeared as cool as when he first attacked. The warrior's thin lips were curved upward slightly, but no warmth reached his eyes. Lightning arced above their heads, and the white light gave the warrior the look of someone already long dead.

The swords met overhead in counterpoint to the thunder, then to the side, and Ty-Sun knew he must do something soon. The two men were evenly matched in strength, but he feared his opponent would wear him down. He would tire long before the other did.

Steadfastly the warrior pushed him back. Ty-Sun could do nothing but give ground. His opponent slashed at him; Ty-Sun feinted then whipped his sword around to the other side and hacked at the warrior. The tip of Dragon's Tongue brushed the warrior's ribs, and his opponent's eyes grew glacial.

Then somehow the warrior tricked Ty-Sun and struck him with the flat of his sword, and the emperor dropped to his knees, his head ringing from the blow. With effort he raised his head and in a flash of lightning saw the descent of the sword. Without thinking, he acted. He rolled aside and then leaped up to his knees and with all his strength drove Dragon's Tongue up at an angle through his opponent's body.

His ice-blue eyes wide, the blond man stared in surprise, then his sword tumbled from his hand. A smell like that of a charnel house issued from the fatal wound, while a hideous keening rose from the bloodless lips. Ty-Sun thrust the blade deeper into the other's body then backed away, covering his nose and mouth with his sleeve.

In horror he watched as his opponent lost control of his legs, toppled over, and started disintegrating. The hair and skin sloughed off first, leaving a leprous-looking white bone that melted, too. Ty-Sun backed away from the foul stench of the body.

When nothing remained of the warrior, he retrieved his sword then wiped the ichor staining the blade onto the ground. He didn't want any touching his clothes or skin. The gods alone knew what would happen then.

Grimly he sheathed Dragon's Tongue. He had defeated one of the Enemy's creatures, and a self-assurance that hadn't been within him for some time returned. It hadn't been easy killing this apparition, but he had done it. And that's what mattered.

Surely this portended the eventual vanquishing of the Enemy.

The white horse pawed at what remained of his master, then rolled his eyes until the whites showed, and galloped off before Ty-Sun could think of capturing him. The horse screamed shrilly, while overhead Ty-Sun heard the other horses answer faintly.

Ty-Sun knew he didn't have enough strength left to fight any of the others, so he closed his eyes, breathed evenly, and within minutes, he knew he was back in the camp once more. He opened his eyes and saw the fire had died down. Martin still slept soundly, his faint snores mixing with the more animated ones of the bear's. Blessing lay on her side wrapped in a blanket against the dampness of the night.

He blinked, then wiped the sweat from his forehead. He was winded and thirsty and very tired. He did not think he would have trouble sleeping tonight; yet he had the next watch.

Soong appeared out of the darkness at that moment. "Your turn now, Your Majesty." Soong warmed his hands over the fire's embers. "I'm surprised, though. I thought you would be sleeping."

"I haven't slept yet this night. I was on the astral plane."

Soong peered closely at him. "What did you find there?"

"An opponent whom I defeated."

"Were that it would be so easy here," Soong said with a weary sigh then lay down by the bear.

Ty-Sun knew when the battle came it would not be as difficult as they feared.

✳— *13* —✳

"I wonder what happened to Lord Elphinstone," Martin mused some days later. "I hope he wasn't injured seriously or killed at the palace. I suppose I'll never know now." He sighed deeply.

"He was indeed a good man," Ty-Sun replied, "and a fine friend for a short time." He closed his eyes again. He'd rested before dinner; they had had a long day in the saddle today, and he was extremely tired. Aware of the boy's silence, he opened one eye.

Martin glanced at him shyly, then ducked his head. "Do you think you could . . . I mean . . . do you think, Your Majesty, you might use that white ball?"

"Do you mean the Orb?"

Martin nodded.

"To see if Lord Elphinstone lives?"

Again Martin nodded, but this time far more vigorously.

"Are you sure? You might not like what the Orb shows you."

"I understand, Your Majesty, but I need to know. I do, indeed."

"Very well." There could be no harm in it, could there, and, too, he was curious as to the fate of this Englishman, a man Blessing claimed held power such as he possessed.

He had never learned all he desired about Lord Elphinstone, but he owed his life and Soong's to the man who had defended them in the ballroom. Ty-Sun took the Orb of White Jade into his hands and began spinning it.

His face intent, Martin squinted, staring into the white depths. "There he is!" He pointed, and Ty-Sun gazed into the jade Orb.

Ty-Sun saw two men on horseback riding across a wide plain dotted with farm fields. The older one had a thin face with plain but comfortable features. He wore his brown hair long with a curled lovelock dangling to one side, and his moustache and small beard were neatly trimmed. His eyes were brown and looked sad, even though at the moment he was chuckling.

Lord Elphinstone was dressed all in yellow with a long coat of bright lemon satin, trunk hose of a saffron hue, and there was even a large plume, dyed gold, waving jauntily from his wide-brimmed hat. Tiny diamonds on the buckles of his shoes and along his cuffs caught the sunlight and glittered. The only other color was the white of his deep lace collar and the lace handkerchief tucked into one side of his sash.

In contrast, the second rider, much younger than Elphinstone and perhaps no older than eighteen or so, wore plain grey breeches and a coat of common cloth and sturdy black shoes with unadorned silver buckles. Clasped around his shoulders was a cloak of the same grey material. He did not appear very tall, but he was lean and looked strong. His eyes were a light brown, his hair thick and of the same shade. He was listening to Lord Elphinstone and nodded in agreement, although he did not smile and laugh as did the other.

"Who is that?" Ty-Sun asked, puzzled. He frowned, trying to remember where he might have seen the boy because he was vaguely familiar. Had they seen him after the shipwreck? In a village?

Soong peered into the Orb, then shrugged and beckoned to Blessing.

"It's my brother, Ned," she said without hesitation. Her surprised expression faded as she drew her eyebrows together. "But where is he, and what is he doing with Lord Elphinstone? I do not think they ever met."

"Perhaps they finally did meet because of the fight in the ballroom that night," Ty-Sun suggested. "You said your brother was not stern in his religion as was your father."

She nodded. "Sometimes I think he always hated our father. Many times when we were children, Ned would protect me, and he would be the one Father ended up taking the strap to. Father tried beating religion into him, but Ned only grew more stubborn. He did not possess the abilities I did, but he was always a loving and kind brother to me."

"Well then, he might have grown disgusted with what your father and Oliver Cromwell did, and so he left England. I would suppose Lord Elphinstone deemed it best to leave, too. As to where they are, well, the land vaguely resembles that area we saw just before we reached the foothills."

"You mean," Soong demanded, "that they're not far from where we were shipwrecked."

"I think not."

"Then they must be following us!" Martin cried. His eyes brightened. "They must be coming to join forces with us, Your Majesty!"

"I think that unlikely, Martin. They could have no way of knowing we were shipwrecked there; nor could they know our course once we set out eastward."

Martin's joyful expression faded. "I suppose you're right, Your Majesty." He stared down at the two men within the Orb for a few minutes more. "We should wait for them then, I think."

Soong clasped the boy on the shoulder and shook his head. "We don't have the time to spare, Martin. They're weeks behind us, and it's likely they wouldn't follow the same path we took."

"Then I'll ride back to meet them."

Soong remained silent but watched Ty-Sun. "You may do that, if you so desire. I would not keep you here, Martin, against your will."

Martin started nodding then stopped. He looked at the Orb, its view of the two riders already fading, then back at Ty-Sun.

"I can't, Your Majesty, as much as I wish to. I gave my word I would serve you."

"But you served Lord Elphinstone first," Ty-Sun pointed out gently.

"Yes, sir, I did, but it's you who needs my service more now. I'll stay."

"Good lad," he said, seeing tears glimmering in the boy's eyes.

❧— 14 —❧

Ty-Sun's confidence increased after his encounter on the astral plane, but even though he was pleased, he did not speak again of his victory to Soong. After all, he knew what the old general would tell him: Ty-Sun was growing too confident, he should be more cautious and prudent, indeed, he should be more like Soong himself. Ty-Sun knew all of this, because Soong had repeated the same tired admonitions numerous times, and he was bored of hearing them.

He wanted to bask in the glow of his victory after so many agonizing setbacks. The defeat of the blond warrior was an achievement he could not have attained half a year ago. No, not even a few weeks ago. And why should he not be proud? This victory betokened a smoother and safer journey for them and ultimately their conquest of the Enemy. He had bested the Enemy once, and he'd do it again!

Soon they would locate this Black Jade Road that Soong carped about, and they would travel like the wind and be back in the Willow Garden before the peach and plum trees blossomed.

He would be only too happy resuming his comfortable existence, replete with fine food and wine and an exceedingly soft bed. How he relished the thought of sleepily reclining in a dragonboat of camphorwood as it drifted across the Willow Lake. His dear concubines would sing to him and caress him and give him sugared almonds. He vowed it would be a long time before he wanted to ride again!

In the days that followed Ty-Sun chatted amiably with the others. He was quick to laugh at Martin's attempts to joke, and he often quoted poetry or would sing an old song. From time to time he would even recite a poem of his own if requested. Ty-Sun was increasingly aware of Soong glancing at him occasionally, but not even the general's fierce expressions could daunt his good humor. He made up an amusing poem about the general, one scarcely flattering although far from malicious, and while the others laughed, Soong merely drew his bushy white eyebrows together thoughtfully.

Day after day passed in this manner until Soong wanted to twist around in the saddle and bluntly tell the emperor to shut up and shop chattering like a magpie. However, he kept his silence, because he knew Ty-Sun would only prattle on.

In truth, it had been a long time since he'd seen his emperor in such a blithe mood. Yet he was bothered by the abrupt change as well, although he didn't know why. Ty-Sun appeared oblivious of any threat to them. Whenever Soong sought to talk to him about arming themselves more heavily, Ty-Sun merely chuckled and promised he would worry about the matter in the morning.

He pulled out the piece of bark upon which he'd been marking the passage of days. A hundred or more since he'd started keeping track. He frowned. It must be close to the summer's end now. Autumn would soon be upon them and then winter, and even though they might be travelling upon the Black Jade Road then, they would also be crossing some of the roughest terrain on their journey home.

This did not bode well.

He could hardly urge them to ride faster, though, for they all were pushed to their limits. The horses were already exhausted as were the riders themselves. No, it would be best if he mentioned nothing, but certainly he would discourage any dawdling. He glanced up at the trees and saw a yellow leaf detach itself and drift slowly downward.

Not a good sign. He thrust it from his mind.

No one in the small company was prepared for the attack when it finally came.

It was close to sunset, and they were all tired from a long day in the saddle. Even Ty-Sun had remained silent for the past hour or more.

Suddenly, men on horseback burst out from the surrounding forest. Several bowmen let arrows loose, and one long arrow found its way to the bridle of Soong's horse. The animal shied, reared and tossed the general to the ground where he lay stunned and unable to rise to his feet.

Ty-Sun glanced down to see if his old friend was all right, then satisfied Soong was far from dead, unsheathed Dragon's Tongue.

Martin held his short sword in readiness while Blessing, her eyes flashing fiercely, gripped her knife, but the riders, numbering close to a score, were among them almost before they could respond and began separating them from each other.

Ty-Sun glanced toward his friends, then he saw no more as they were surrounded.

Mud and ash daubed the faces of the attackers, while twigs and clumps of dirt clung to their torn and soiled clothing. Ty-Sun considered it odd that neither the swordsmen nor the horses had made a sound since appearing. The whites of the horses' eyes gleamed in the faint light as if they were afraid.

Soong had gained his feet and now fought with a sword Martin had tossed him. A confident smile tugging at his lips, Ty-Sun lay about left and right with Dragon's Tongue, slashing at those rushing him. One man toppled from the saddle, and the horse fled in terror.

Another soldier tried running Ty-Sun through, but he ducked low, then swung his horse around and rammed his sword into the man's chest. He pulled it out quickly, then kicked the roan forward. He cut and hacked at the swordsmen, all the while dodging the hail of arrows. One bit into the fleshy part of his arm, and grabbing the arrow, he pulled it out and tossed it away. The forest floor was littered now with their opponents' bodies, and still the men fought on.

Ty-Sun brought the flat of Dragon's Tongue down across an archer ready to release another arrow, then he glanced at Martin to see how the youth was doing. The boy had found another sword, this one long and deadly-looking, and he faced his opponents with two blades now. Soong let out a war cry, followed by the sound of a horse's hooves thundering through the forest.

The bear, who had been cowering behind a bush dark with berries, roared and rose to his full height, and with one swipe of a mighty paw brought another swordsman down. The horse screamed and fled while the bear growled after it.

Ty-Sun ran another attacker through then looked to see how Blessing fared. He couldn't see her in the melee, and he wondered if she'd been knocked from her saddle. She might need his help. He wheeled his mount around, kicked a man struggling to his feet out of the way then spun the horse around once more. He still couldn't see her.

"Blessing!"

Over the sound of clashing arms and the grunts of his comrades, he thought he heard a faint cry. A woman's voice.

He knew then what had happened and how the swordsmen had tricked them.

"She's gone. They've taken her!" Ty-Sun yelled to his companions.

He kicked his horse forward, but the animal was cut off immediately. He raised his sword, bringing it down across the shoulder of first one man, then another. He slashed at them and kicked them as they tried grabbing his mount, and all the while he cursed his stupidity. When he was free, he spurred the horse and rode in the direction from which the cry had come, but it was too late. He neither saw nor heard anything, and the last bit of light had fled, plunging the forest into darkness. He returned to find Soong and Martin alone, their attackers having left as well.

"No sign of Blessing?" Soong asked. He was wiping his stained sword.

"No. We must ride after them. I think I know which direction they took."

Martin helped Soong into the saddle, then caught his own horse by the bridle and hoisted himself into the saddle.

A muffled bark rose from a pocket, and Ty-Sun peered in at an annoyed Ch'u. He took the dog out and stroked his head as he glanced around for the cat. However, he did not see her and wondered if the feline had gone in search of her mistress. As for the bear . . . he heard a crash in the trees to his right and then relaxed as the bear lumbered into sight.

He returned the dog to his pocket, then caught the reins of Blessing's horse and tied it to the rope leading the pack horse.

"What was wrong with those men, General Soong?" Martin asked. "They never made a sound during the entire battle, and their faces were horrible. I've never seen anything like that."

"They were dead men, I think. Raised from their graves by the Enemy to do his bidding. That accounts for the mud and bits of earth."

Shivering, Martin hastily crossed himself. " 'Twas an unholy crew that. God alone knows what they'll send us next."

"It's almost nightfall, Your Majesty," Soong said softly, watching Ty-Sun as he surveyed the quiet forest. "Perhaps we should wait until morning to start tracking her."

"No, we cannot delay. We must go now before the trail grows too cold. My own conceit and dull wits allowed this to happen, and I fear what they might do to Blessing before we reach them."

Soong glanced at Martin, who fell in behind him, the two extra horses in tow, and they began riding through the dark forest.

They did not find Blessing.

Riding daily from before dawn to well after nightfall, the three men searched through the forest, but found no trail indicating where the dead men might have taken Blessing. They rode until they were so exhausted they were nearly falling from their saddles, but still they came across no sign, and in that time, no one threatened them. Even the black birds which had spied constantly on them had disappeared.

Secretly Martin was having doubts they would ever locate Blessing, but he did not voice this opinion. Instead, he kept his mouth shut and rode where the emperor directed him.

"I don't understand," Ty-Sun said nearly a week later as they camped. "I thought the Enemy would press his advantage. We are reduced by one and very nearly lost that skirmish. I'm surprised he hasn't sent other soldiers our way. We're so exhausted that I fear it wouldn't take much to defeat us."

Martin nodded and gulped down a mouthful of fresh water to soften the dried meat he was chewing. He broke off a small piece and fed it to Ch'u. They'd not seen the cat since Blessing's disappearance, and he wondered if the animal had proven a casualty of the battle. He truly hoped not.

"Perhaps," Soong replied, "it was not you the Enemy wanted, after all."

"Explain yourself, greybeard."

"Look into your heart for the answer, my lord." He walked away.

Irritated, Ty-Sun left the campfire. Ch'u trotted after him. As he reached the closest trees, Ty-Sun looked back at the camp, then shrugged.

What did Soong mean by his cryptic remark? What *was* he to make of this? The Enemy had spirited Blessing away, and in all that time Ty-Sun and his friends had not been attacked, nor had they been spied upon. Which could mean only one thing.

The true object of each attack had never been himself, as he imagined, but Blessing.

It was a blow to his ego; yet he knew it was true. Blessing was the key, no one else. Had he not crossed half the world to find her, to take her back to the Land of Ten Thousand Willows to become his bride? Now the Enemy had found a way to take her from him.

Why?

Because without his bride and their ultimate marriage, Ty-Sun could do nothing. He was powerless to stop the onslaught of the Enemy and his evil minions. Helpless to prevent the destruction of his beloved dragons and the

Willow Garden and, ultimately, the world in which they lived.

Everything depended upon Blessing, and now she was gone.

Long ago Soong must have seen this, but he'd wanted Ty-Sun to discover it himself. Soong should have told him, he thought defensively, and yet, would he have believed his own friend? No. He'd had to delve into his heart for the solution to Soong's riddle, and he found something else within it as well.

He found foolishness and pride and conceit—all destructive. To think he could so easily defeat the Enemy in that mock battle on the astral plane. The blond warrior had merely been a diversion; the Enemy had known he would lessen his guard thereafter, and so he had. That was when the Enemy would strike.

Blessing was gone, thanks to him as much as to the Enemy.

He stooped and picked up the small dog and stroked its silky fur. He was a fool, a dangerous fool for the woman he loved.

"But I will find her," he whispered to Ch'u, "I will save her and make amends. Upon that, my friend, you have my solemn word."

PART II

❧— *15* —❧

Lord Jindrich Vlastenecký had slept far too long, and now the sun was fast sinking in the sky. That meant darkness would soon cover the forest, and the night spirits would roam freely through their black domain. For over two days now he'd travelled without resting and, exhausted, had finally lain down under a tree. He had just closed his eyes for a minute, but that minute had stretched into hours.

Even worse, he'd selected a spot close to a stream. The *vodyanoi*, or water spirits, waited for those like him, foolish enough to fall asleep by a lake or river or stream. Often under cover of darkness the *vodyanoi* would creep up on an unwary traveller, fasten him securely, and the next thing the human knew he would be the main course of the water spirits' meals.

He seized his sword and, scrambling to his feet, brushed leaves and twigs from his clothes. He must leave at once.

"Not so fast, *lidsky*," hissed a wet-sounding voice from behind him.

Vlastenecký, sword fast in his hand, whirled around to see one of the spirits advancing on him. To his left was another, to his right two more, and behind him now several others had sneaked up quietly. In other words, he was surrounded by the creatures. If there had only been one or two facing him, he knew he would have no trouble; but to have more than a half dozen . . . well, the odds didn't favor him.

As tall as a fully-grown man, the *vodyanoi* resembled humans except their skin was the green of newly scythed grass. They wore their black hair in two long plaits, and droplets of water dripped down their sleek bodies. They possessed iridescent eyes, round and lidless, a mouth full of honed teeth, and a ridge of deadly-looking, rusty spines ran along the outside of their arms and the center of their backs.

It was claimed that any human scratched by those sharp spines containing terrible poison would die horribly, a far worse death than being eaten by the creatures. Hardly a good fate.

Vlastenecký well knew the legend that went hand-in-hand with the creatures. Once, long ago, a beautiful maiden who was spurned by her lover decided to throw herself into a lake. As she plunged into the water, though, a fish caught her, saving her life, and because her life now belonged to him, he took her to live in his crystal palace at the bottom of the lake. There she lived more than a century and bore him many sons and daughters, the first of the race of the *vodyanoi*. If indeed they had ever had a human ancestor, it meant nothing to them.

Lidsky.

How ugly they could make the word "human" sound, he thought.

"*Lidsky*, you will die now." The water spirit gnashed his long teeth then leered.

"We shall see about that," Vlastenecký muttered. He decided not to let them make the first move and rushed the nearest creature.

It hissed at him and tried dodging, but his sword caught

it in the side, ripping away a handful of spines. Clear liquid pumped from the body as Vlastenecký jumped back so the stuff wouldn't splash him.

The others surged toward him as he whirled, hacking at one, then another. All the while he reminded himself to stay clear of the spines.

Their breathing rasped on him, cold and unpleasant, and he thrust his sword at one, then pulled it out and tried hacking at another. But the creature nimbly leaped out of danger.

Suddenly beyond in the forest he heard sounds of horsemen and wondered what new devilment was coming. Then abruptly three horsemen burst into the clearing. One white-haired man was yelling and letting loose arrows that whistled as they sped through the air to find their targets. A *vodyanoi* pitched forward, two arrows in the tender spots of his back. A second man on horseback used a great sword that seemed to gleam with a light of its own, while a third man, much younger than the others, busied himself with a water spirit that now charged him.

Within minutes none of the *vodyanoi* remained alive. Short of breath, Vlastenecký rested his crossed arms atop his sword and studied his rescuers. Two wore the most unusual clothing he had ever seen, but the youngest dressed much like him.

"I thank you, strangers," he said in a dialect of Latin.

The white-haired man spoke. "You are most welcome, sir." The man stared down at the corpses. "What manner of creatures were those?"

"They're called *vodyanoi* and are spirits found in lakes and rivers. They lie in wait for unsuspecting travellers."

The tall man, who had not yet spoken now asked, as he eyed the stream dubiously, "Are we safe here? Or will more of those things attack?"

Vlastenecký shook his head. "The others have seen that to go against us is futile, so they'll stay in the water and wait for someone else." He straightened. "I forget my manners. Allow me to introduce myself. I am Lord Jindrich Vlastenecký." He bowed low.

Ty-Sun introduced himself and his two friends, then studied the man whom they'd rescued. He stood above average height with a stocky frame, although he was by no means heavy. Gold streaked his chestnut-colored hair that was cropped close and had not been combed recently, and his eyes were quite odd—a light brown with yellow flecks.

His face was darkened, as though he spent much time out of doors, while his high cheekbones and narrow face gave him an intriguing look. He wore leather breeches, a stained shirt once white with cuffs that ended in elaborate lace now torn, and a long brown coat, heavily embroidered with a row of brass buttons down its entire length. His shoes were heavy leather and muddy, and he had a knife sheathed at his side.

"Thank you again for your timely help. It would have been a long hard fight."

"And your last one, at that," said Soong with a slight twist of his lips.

Vlastenecký grinned. "Aye, it would have been. Now how might I repay you, gentlemen?"

"Perhaps you can give us some information we seek," Ty-Sun said.

"Anything within my power."

"I suggest, Your Majesty," said Martin, eyeing the water nervously, "that we leave this stream and find a good location for camp."

"An excellent idea," Soong agreed.

They located a site not far away and there made camp for the night. As they ate, they talked with Lord Vlastenecký.

"You are in the land of Bohemia now where dark times have fallen."

"Oh?" Soong leaned forward with interest.

"For centuries my country has been torn between its different religions. The opposing sects war constantly against one another, although from time to time there have been truces. As it happens, I am not of the two major religions—neither Roman Catholic nor Protestant. I am what might be termed a pagan." He watched them, and when he saw interest, he proceeded. "For many years I maintained good relations with my neighbors, many of them Catholics, but recently that changed.

"It was as if someone were driving a wedge between us. Protestants gathered on one side, Catholics on the other, and the fighting renewed. It concerned small matters at first—a squabble about a boundary or rightful ownership of wandering cows. Slowly it worsened, and then the Germans and the mercenaries flooded into my land, and open war erupted. Because I still tried talking reason with my neighbors and those who fought bitterly, I was branded a heretic. My wife and children were killed, my lands were seized, and I was forced to flee."

"And since then?" Martin prompted.

"I've wandered the land helping those other unfortunates when I can. Brigands and such abound now, and much work can be found. Too, wildlife is abundant here, and I never lack for food." He finished his stew. "Now what about you?"

In as few words as possible and even then it took some time to fully relate, Ty-Sun told him of their journey from the Land of Ten Thousand Willows, and how they found themselves in Bohemia and would soon be searching for the Black Jade Road.

At tale's end, Vlastenecký rocked back and stared in amazement at them.

"If you did not look like honest men, I would think you had spun a fairy tale for me."

"I fear it's all too true," Soong grunted.

"Alas, yes, and now we seek the whereabouts of my bride-to-be. The information we ask of you is this—have you seen a red-haired woman of late? We believe she might have been brought this way."

"A red-haired woman, eh?" Vlastenecký stroked the stubble on his chin. "It's rumored that women with hair the color of flames can converse with animals, although that just might be legend." Ty-Sun and Soong exchanged looks. "I've not seen one, but there is someplace where you might check. I've seen it from afar, and there are strange goings-on there. Many soldiers arrive and leave, and I think it's the center of the disturbances in my land."

"Sounds like the hand of the Enemy again, " Soong said, while Martin merely nodded.

"Could you take us there?"

"Yes, but the way is dangerous."

"Our way has been fraught with dangers since the day we stepped out of the Willow Garden. I have no fear of perils."

"Very well. Tomorrow we'll head back toward my castle. You may stay there for a while, but I fear the accommodations are poor."

"In a castle?" Martin asked. How could that be? Didn't everyone know that castles were magnificent? Why, Lord Elphinstone had had an ancestral castle surrounded by groves of old oaks, and hadn't that been the most wonderful place? Martin sighed and closed his eyes. Sometimes he wanted very much to be home in England. But, he told himself briskly, he couldn't. He'd made his choice, and he would stand by it. Lord Elphinstone would think that only right.

"You'll see when you arrive," Vlastenecký said with a faint smile.

Suddenly something crashed through the bushes and roared loudly, the sound echoing. Growling all the while, the bear lumbered toward them. Vlastenecký leaped to his feet, his sword in his hand, and looked bewildered when the other men remained sitting.

"A bear!" the man exclaimed. "We must defend ourselves!"

Ty-Sun smiled slightly, while Soong and Martin merely chuckled. Martin rose and dished some stew into a pan and took it to the bear, who rubbed his shaggy head against the boy's arm.

Vlastenecký gaped in amazement.

The others were laughing openly now, and when Ty-Sun caught his breath, he said, "I think it's best I elaborate a few details of my story." And he indicated for the Bohemian lord to sit.

The next day they broke camp early.

"We won't have far to ride today," Vlastenecký said. Riding Blessing's horse, he led the way through the dense forest.

"Good," murmured Ty-Sun. He ached all over, but then these days he never seemed to stop being sore. Perhaps if he spent a few days out of the saddle he might have a chance to recover.

Martin gazed around with interest at the thick woods that were different from the others through which they'd gone. They didn't seem as dark or menacing, he supposed, and yet the trees looked ancient, as if they had stood here from the beginning of time. Some reminded him of his former master's favorite tree in London, a great oak Lord Elphinstone claimed was the oldest tree in all Britain and a holy one at that. But then Lord Elphinstone was a bit odd, Martin reflected, considering he was a Druid or something like that.

The emperor and Lord Vlastenecký were talking a lot today. Vlastenecký told them about his life in the castle which Martin found exceedingly interesting, and then the emperor countered with exotic tales of his own country. Soong, though, kept his silence while the other two chattered.

It was just like they were all out for a simple ride through the woods.

Still, Martin remained more than a little uneasy. He fully expected those disgusting water spirits to jump out at them every time they forded a river or circled a pond. And Lord Vlastenecký claimed they ate human flesh. Martin shook his head. He had never heard such a thing. Just wait until Lord Elphinstone heard about the *vodyanoi*. Wouldn't he just be amazed?

Ch'u was fairly fidgety, too. The small dog rode with him today instead of his usual place in the emperor's pocket, and the dog kept glancing back in the direction from which they'd just come or to one side and then up at Martin's face as if trying to tell him something.

Occasionally he whined and licked his nose nervously while his round eyes bulged. To reassure him Martin stroked the dog's soft fur and felt the tiny body trembling.

"It's all right, boy," he whispered. "I don't think anything's going to happen. At least not until we find Mistress Blessing."

Ch'u only whimpered; beside them the bear raised his snout and moaned.

The black dog loped gracefully across the forest floor, keeping easy pace with the horsemen. Every so often a growl rose from deep in his throat. He had the blood scent in his nose, and from far ahead he sensed the tremulous beating of the tiny dog's heart. The other would scarcely make a meal for him. Saliva dripped from his strong jaws as he imagined springing forward and bringing the horse down, biting through the man's neck and seizing the tiny dog. He could taste the warm blood.

The other dog and the bear sensed they were being

followed, and the black hound would have smiled, if capable.

He would continue following the four horsemen, and when the right moment came, he would quicken his pace and attack.

He would leap and knock the last rider—the nervous one—out of the saddle and kill him and the other dog and the horse, too, if it didn't run off, all before the other riders were alerted, or before the bear turned on him. Yet he had seen the bear hide from danger before, and he was confident the same thing would recur. Then he would dart back into the forest and follow them, waiting for the next opportunity.

"Your Majesty!" Martin called softly.

Ty-Sun glanced back over his shoulder. "What is it, Martin?"

"I think something's wrong."

Ty-Sun waited until Martin reached his side, then studied the forest. "What makes you think that?"

"I don't know. I just sense it, and poor little Ch'u here is agitated. And look at the bear."

Ty-Sun stared at the dog, who trembled so hard it was a wonder he hadn't fallen off the horse. Martin held him onto the saddle with one hand that also could stroke him to calm him down. The bear kept swinging his muzzle from left to right as if trying to catch a scent.

"Soong."

The general rode back. "Yes?"

"Do you sense anything wrong?" Soong raised a bushy eyebrow. "Take a look at the animals."

The old man studied them, then looked back at the woods. He thought he detected a shadow move suddenly, but he wasn't sure.

"We won't take any chances," he said. "Take out your weapons."

Ty-Sun took Ch'u and slipped him into his pocket so that Martin could free his hand for his sword, and their small group edged closer together.

The dog bared its fangs in savage disappointment. The horsemen suspected something was wrong, and so he couldn't attack now.

Well, he would just have to wait until they were lulled once more. He would wait as long as needed. He was, after all, exceedingly patient.

Vlastenecký and the others reached the castle late that afternoon. Atop a hill, its jagged ruins were black against the pale sky.

"My former home." Bitterness twisted his face and tone.

As they rode up the incline, they stared at the fortress. None of the outer grey stone walls stood unscathed; great gaping holes poked through the front, while in several places the walls looked as though they had simply crumbled. The portcullis had been torn down from the gateway and left to rust.

In many places Ty-Sun and Soong spotted long black scars, evidence the castle had been put to the torch as well. Undergrowth had crept from the forest to the ruins, and vines with profuse purple and white blossoms crawled up those walls still partially standing.

The four horsemen rode through the gateway, then dismounted and tied the horses to fallen timbers. Ty-Sun turned and looked around. The inner wall, or rampart, had suffered just as much as the outer wall; numerous battlements had been knocked down so that they lay broken in pieces at the foot of the wall. He was surprised to see several towers had escaped the fury of the nobleman's enemies.

From there they passed into the keep. Ty-Sun stared at what had once been the great hall. A partially charred tapestry still hung on one scorched wall, and broken crockery lay in a heap near his feet. Here and there he saw the glint of glass or something metallic, while along one wall he spotted bleached bones. Weeds and vines had entered here, too, and green covered nearly everything inside the keep.

He imagined how it must have appeared before the destruction: colorful banners hanging from the galley at the hall's end where musicians played merrily and a roaring fire in the massive fireplace; servants running back and forth serving their lord and lady, both dressed in fine silks and lace and velvets, and the lord himself with his family seated around him conversing with several travellers who had stopped for the night.

His impression was that the nobleman was truly impartial as well as educated. He could well guess at the conversations in the great hall, too. Religion and philosophy, poetry, mathematics, and astronomy—with Lord Vlastenecký encouraging discussion and expansion of knowledge. Was it any wonder that his small-minded neighbors had hated such a man?

Clouds of dust puffed upward as they stepped through the ruins. Occasionally they spotted a bird's nest perched precariously high on a wall. A slight wind, forecasting the impending chilly night, blew, bringing with it the perfume of newly opened flowers.

A sad and lonely place, Ty-Sun mused. Desolate in body and mind, and when he glanced at Vlastenecký, he saw tears in the man's eyes.

Opposite, a stone stairway led upward to a single tower left unscathed.

Vlastenecký pointed upward. "What I wanted to show you, you can see from there."

Ty-Sun nodded and stepped carefully across the littered floor, once white marble, now brown with a stain he knew was blood shed by the family here long ago. He came to the stairway and began climbing. He lost count of the steps after one hundred then simply concentrated on reaching the top.

Here the breeze became a brisk wind, and he held onto a stone to maintain his balance. In one dusty corner lay an old discarded bird's nest, the remnants of shells and a small decayed form still there.

Ty-Sun gazed outward. There was the forest through which they had so recently travelled, and as far as he could see in that westerly direction, there were trees, dark and thick and unbroken. Beyond, though, on the horizon, he saw farmland, and toward the south he saw fields lying much closer. To the north lay still more trees, and to the east—

He squinted in the fading sunlight, not sure what he saw. He was exhausted, having ridden a long way today. So, that must be it. Or was it simply some odd trick of light?

"Soong!" he called. "Come up here at once. You must see this."

"I'm coming!"

Within moments Ty-Sun heard the other's approach. Soon the general stood by his side, his breath puffing ever so slightly.

"What's so important I must traipse up here?" he grumbled.

"Look there," Ty-Sun said, pointing. "Tell me what you see."

Obligingly Soong gazed eastward out across the trees then thoughtfully stroked his moustache. He glanced at Ty-Sun, then eastward, and muttered something under his breath.

"Well?" Ty-Sun asked impatiently.

"Looks like a tree."

"Yes, yes, I know, but, old friend, what sort of tree is it that can be seen so clearly? It must be hundred *li* distant."

"That's true."

"You see it, then?"

It was Vlastenecký, who had come up behind them so quietly they hadn't heard him.

"The tree, yes," replied Ty-Sun. "It cannot be natural."

"Indeed, it isn't," said the nobleman. "I remember a time when it wasn't there."

Soong's white eyebrows drew together in a frown. "Then how did it come to be there? Did it simply appear one day?"

"I know that sounds impossible, but yes, it did. One morning I rose to the sound of my guards calling me up here, and I saw the same thing you do now. Like you, I wondered about it, but already it was too late for shortly afterward all our troubles started."

"It's built by the Enemy," Ty-Sun murmured, secure in his knowledge, while his hands tightened until the knuckles were white.

"Yes," said Soong.

And where the Enemy might be, Ty-Sun reasoned, could he not hope to find Blessing?

⟫⟩⟨ 17 ⟨⟩⟫

The tree was the color of ebony. Sunlight glinted off leaves as black as the trunk, which stood perfectly straight. Not even the wind rustled those dark leaves. It dwarfed the trees surrounding it. Above all, it was unnatural.

Shivering as he gazed at the black tree, Ty-Sun remembered the black spire which he'd seen that first time upon the astral plane. The Enemy was here as in the spire. He was sure of it.

The three men returned to the keep where they told Martin what they'd seen.

He crossed himself quickly.

"We cannot foolishly rush off yet," Soong said as he sat on a stone that had long ago tumbled from the wall. Ch'u leaped into his lap, and absently he stroked the tiny animal.

"How do we prepare for something like that?" Ty-Sun demanded.

"I don't know," the general replied honestly.

Ty-Sun gave an exasperated sigh.

Soong scowled. "I think we should first scout the area. There might be soldiers there. Indeed, Lord Vlastenecký, you mentioned that you've seen soldiers coming and going from there before." The nobleman nodded. "We watch for a day or two to establish the pattern, if any, and then we sit down and make our plans."

131

"We don't have days," Ty-Sun said.

Soong continued. "Your Majesty, we've waited this long. Another day or two won't matter much, especially if a slight delay will prevent us from running headlong into some unfortunate disaster."

Ty-Sun did not reply.

"I think two of us must observe the tree closely while the other two stay here." Soong glanced at the others.

"I'll go," Ty-Sun volunteered immediately.

Martin shook his head. "I'm sorry, Your Majesty, but I don't think either you or the general should go. If anyone must, then I'll do it. You're too valuable to lose."

"I agree," Soong said.

"Precisely. That's why I'll go with the boy," Vlastenecký said. "However, I think Martin and I should leave soon. I have no idea how long it will take, and I think the sooner we reach it the better. And it's better to arrive there in darkness without the benefit of many eyes on us."

Soong nodded. "All right. We'll give you some food, and then you can be on your way."

The men ate a hasty meal, divided some provisions for the scouts, then Vlastenecký and Martin mounted their horses and promised they'd return within two days' time. If they did not return by then, Soong and Ty-Sun must assume the worst.

Martin and Vlastenecký crouched behind a rotting log and gazed at the black tree. Only a hundred yards away now, they saw its base was nearly the size of Vlastenecký's ruined castle. When they looked upward they lost sight of the strange tree where it broke through the canopy of much smaller trees. The burnished trunk was smooth, almost like a black stone, and completely devoid of branches or openings.

Since their arrival in the night, they had watched the tree.

Nothing had happened until shortly after dawn when the two scouts saw a number of foot soldiers patrolling around the tree. Some had left shortly after that, but still the area was heavily guarded. Several soldiers on horseback had arrived a short time ago, and they, too, patrolled.

Which must mean, the young man reasoned, that there must be something in there worth protecting. But how could anything—or anyone, for that matter—be in that tree? There was no way to enter, as far as he could detect.

"What do we tell the emperor?" he whispered to his companion. "There's a dozen soldiers for each of us and maybe more. They keep coming and going so there's no way to count them. Besides, we can't fight all of them—no matter that the Emperor can use his magic—and as far as I can see, your lordship, there's no way into the blasted thing."

"Perhaps there is an entrance on the other side, one that we haven't seen yet. I'll take a quick look," Vlastenecký said, restraining a smile. "You wait for me here, Martin."

Martin only nodded and wished with all his heart that they could simply find Mistress Blessing and be done with this strange tree. He didn't like it one bit.

Vlastenecký slipped past several soldiers in leather armor who stood too engrossed in noisy conversation to be listening carefully and angled toward the left. What he had seen so far didn't bode well. The trunk remained smooth on all sides. But there was one part that he hadn't investigated yet.

A twig snapped under his foot, and he paused as a soldier twisted around. The man seemed to stare directly at him, but Vlastenecký knew he hadn't been seen. Breath caught, he waited until the soldier resumed his conversation with his fellows then slowly slid across the ground.

Now almost opposite where he and Martin had watched for so long, he still saw no way in. Perhaps they'd overlooked something such as an underground entrance. Yet the soldiers never entered the tree, so that seemed doubtful.

Vlastenecký scratched his head, and considered the strange black tree just a small part of the puzzle that was the Enemy. The Enemy . . . he'd seen its form many times, long before he knew there existed one single opponent drawing power from those it crushed.

He had seen friends and neighbors turn against him and his family, had seen his loved ones killed, his belongings scattered to the winds. His devoted servants and friends had been imprisoned, and he knew it was unlikely he would ever see them again. His land, his country, had been raped, all in the name of the Enemy.

The Enemy.

Vlastenecký spat.

Early the next morning the scouts returned to the castle and reported very little.

"There must be a way in, though," Ty-Sun mused as he paced before the others. "Why else would the tree be where it is?"

"Perhaps it serves to tempt you or to divert your attention from something else. Who can say what goes on in the Enemy's mind?" Soong asked.

Without replying, Ty-Sun continued pacing. His hands were clasped loosely behind his back. Soong noted, as he had before, that his lord's fingernails, once long and cased in silver sheaths which clicked musically as he moved his fingers, were now short and bluntly cut, the nails broken off.

Where was the pampered, hopeless monarch of a year ago? Soong prayed that man had disappeared forever. Ty-Sun, he knew, was becoming more like other men which was not a bad thing. Ty-Sun would never be common, but he had to learn certain things. Humility—and patience— were just two of them.

"While you were gone the Emperor used the Orb of White Jade to locate Blessing."

Martin leaned forward eagerly. "Yes? What did you see, Your Majesty? Did you see Mistress Blessing? Is she all right? Where is she?"

Soong shook his head. "I fear we both saw only darkness." Martin's eager expression faded. "She could be alive or dead. We don't know."

A heavy silence fell among the men, finally broken by Ty-Sun.

"She's there, I know it. I will find a way into that tree, and I will rescue her. No matter what it takes, or how long."

Blessing lay in the darkness, or at least she assumed she was lying. Perhaps she stood. She couldn't be sure. All she knew was she could move neither her feet nor arms; not even her head, and that frightened her. She was not blindfolded; she was simply in darkness, a black without relief. She was never too cold or too warm, and the cell, if it were that, wasn't damp which was a relief. From time to time, food, bland but adequate, was provided, but she never saw who brought it. She only felt the none-too-gentle hands and the spoon at her mouth, and she ate, knowing she needed her strength.

The rest of the endless dark time she waited. Would Ty-Sun come to rescue her? Yet how could he know where she had been taken? She didn't know that herself. She'd tried to watch where they were going, but the trees blurred by and then darkness came, and she was here in this strange place.

And worse—as time slipped by, she could not rid herself of this notion—what if he'd been killed by those men who'd taken her? What if now his body lay far away in that forest?

She could not bear to consider it, yet the terrible images remained burned in her mind. Or what if he were alive and he searched and searched and searched but couldn't find her?

Some time later she fell asleep. She slept a lot because it helped pass the time. Sometimes she spoke aloud to herself or sang, but her voice echoed so much she stopped, the ringing finally dying away.

"I love you, Ty-Sun," she whispered aloud as she closed her eyes to wait.

✕⊷— *18* —⊷✕

The four men arrived late the next afternoon, and both Soong and Ty-Sun stared in awe at the sight. Natural or not, it was truly incredible. A beautiful, unblemished ebony, the tree was so cold-looking Ty-Sun suspected it would feel like ice if he placed his hand upon the trunk. It was almost a work of art, and for a moment he could almost forget who the artist was.

The soldiers still swarmed like ants about the tree, making closer inspection impossible. They waited over an hour for the soldiers to depart, but none did. Ty-Sun and Soong circled the tree as had Vlastenecký, but they saw no openings.

How did anyone enter it? Ty-Sun asked himself in frustration. Surely there must be an entrance. Yet, how did he know it was hollow? It was so huge, though, that it must do more than simply act as a base for these soldiers, and also, if it were simply a solid tree, why would it be so closely guarded?

No, there was something or someone in there. Now it was just a matter of entering it. Dejected, he sat on the ground and stared glumly at the tree. A smooth puzzle whose key was beyond his comprehension.

"What about the Orb of White Jade?" Martin asked in a whisper.

"What?" Ty-Sun glanced up, startled.

"Can't you use the Orb to find a way into the tree, Your Majesty? You mentioned before that you met up with the Enemy's soldiers when you spun the Orb. Well, perhaps now that you're at the tree, there might be a tree on that plane."

"Martin," Ty-Sun said slowly, "I think you might just be right."

The boy grinned.

Ty-Sun lifted the Orb from a pocket. He gazed at the ball, then at Soong, who crept closer.

"When I'm in the trance you must guard me carefully, Soong. There exists a far greater danger in using magic this close to the tree; it could well attract the Enemy's attention, but it's something I must risk."

Soong nodded. Vlastenecký stared at the Orb; he had never seen anything like it.

Ty-Sun smiled grimly, noting the other's interest. "It'll help me fall into a trance."

"A trance," the Bohemian repeated as if he'd never heard the word before.

"Yes." Ty-Sun held the Orb carefully. "When we first met you, Lord Vlastenecký, you said you were a pagan. What sort? There seem to be many. Lord Elphinstone, Martin's former master, is a Druid, and they worship trees, I understand; my Blessing is a witch—not an evil one, that is. As a pagan, what do you believe?"

"In good and evil."

"Don't all religions believe in that?" Martin asked quietly. "Mine does."

"Most do, but not all practice it," the nobleman said. "All in the world can be divided into good or bad, and you must do good while you live, or you will burn in a terrible hell."

"Interesting," Ty-Sun murmured. "The yin-yang is similar—without the burning in hell, of course." And briefly he outlined to Vlastenecký the principle of the two major opposing forces of the universe.

Vlastenecký nodded slowly. "Light and dark, male and female, sun and moon, summer and winter. I think I must have always believed in this yin-yang. But which is which?"

"The yang is the male principle, the yin is the female," Soong explained. "But enough of this, or those soldiers will soon be breathing down our necks. Are you ready, Your Majesty?"

He nodded, and Martin and Vlastenecký closed in around Ty-Sun with their weapons in hand as he spun the Orb. He stared at it, watching the light play off the white jade. Specks of light danced in front of his eyes then coalesced, and the Orb began glistening. He found himself growing lighter and lighter until he felt as if he were floating, and then abruptly he tumbled down a long, black shaft. When he reached the bottom, he stared up and saw the normal sky, yet when he glanced away, he saw he was once more on the astral plane.

This time the plane was not empty. Ahead stood the tree as huge and black and impassive as in the other world. Here no soldiers guarded it; all that could be seen on the plane was the tree and him.

And once more no entrance.

Anger and frustration roiled within him, and gripping the astral Dragon's Tongue firmly, Ty-Sun strode forward until only a few feet from the tree's trunk. Violently he swung the sword. As the metal hit the tree, blue and white sparks flew, and he heard a high-pitched humming, and the tree swallowed the sword. Frowning, he withdrew the sword then touched the scored place; his hand disappeared. He pulled it out then repeated the action. The same thing happened. Understanding at last, he smiled.

There had always been an entrance, but their minds had been clouded by the Enemy. And thus as hard as they might search, they could not find it.

Taking a deep breath and praying to the silent gods for strength, Ty-Sun lifted Dragon's Tongue and stepped through the black trunk.

"He hasn't moved at all since he fell asleep," Martin whispered. It was uncanny how still the emperor was; not a muscle, not an eyelid had twitched since he'd closed his eyes. Sometimes Martin wasn't even sure Ty-Sun was breathing.

"Nor will he again until he comes out of the trance," Soong explained.

Martin shook his head. " 'Tis a strange thing, this, but a good one, I wager."

"Yes." Soong studied the soldiers guarding the tree. Nothing had changed, and he wondered if Ty-Sun had entered yet. "Even if the emperor is successful, though, and rescues Blessing, our journey is still not over."

"What?"

Soong smiled slightly. "Have you forgotten the Black Jade Road, Martin? We still must find that so we may return to the Willow Garden."

Martin could find nothing to say.

Ty-Sun took a step forward into a blackness, far darker and more complete than anything he'd ever encountered. It was like a velvet cloth clinging and smothering him, and without moving any farther, he raised the astral Orb so the light it cast would break the cloth's hold.

He found an immense chamber, almost as large as

Vlastenecký's ruined castle. Completely devoid of any ornamentation, the room possessed a wall and floor as black as the tree's exterior. He brushed a hand against a section of wall nearest him and snatched it back when coldness bit into his fingertips. A tree hewn from black ice.

In the center he saw a free-standing circular staircase so narrow no more than two men abreast could ascend at the same time. He looked up where the steps led, but darkness shrouded its upper reaches. Nowhere did he see any doors.

Ty-Sun prepared to take a step forward when suddenly he paused. Something made him mistrust the floor. Carefully he grazed the floor with the tip of his sword. It disappeared. Puzzled, he withdrew the weapon, then searched in his pockets for a small object. He found a round stone Ch'u had fetched one day and tossed it onto the floor. The stone sank immediately, and Ty-Sun listened for it to strike the bottom of this mysterious abyss. He heard nothing.

It could well have been him dropping like that stone. A close call, he realized, as he released his breath slowly. Apparently he stood on a small ledge ringing the room, although he couldn't be sure it continued the entire way around. If an abyss existed in front, cleverly disguised as a floor, then how would he cross to the stairs?

Some way must exist, or else there wouldn't be stairs. Right? Not unless the Enemy and his servants could all fly.

He stooped and saw something like a beam, darker than the floor, slightly to one side of where he would have initially stepped. Once more using his sword, he found the plank solid. He slid his sword across until his arm fully extended, and he calculated the beam stretched toward the center. He straightened and saw then that there were other beams, all radiating from the stairs like the spokes of a wheel. The distance from beam to beam was nearly the length of his sword.

His way across the abyss.

Ty-Sun sheathed Dragon's Tongue because he would need his arms for balance. The beam didn't appear much wider than his foot, so he tucked the Orb into a pocket as well. Then he stepped onto the nearest beam. In a matter of minutes, provided he didn't overbalance, he would be standing at the base of the stairs.

His expression froze. Was he moving? He wet a finger, raised it, knew then the beam was rotating to his right. He took a step forward, felt the beam tremble and accelerate beneath him ever so slightly. Another step, and still faster. At the rate he was going, by the time he was halfway across the beam, it would be spinning so fast he couldn't stay balanced atop it.

What could he do?

Slowly he dropped to his knees and inched carefully forward. His body swayed precariously from the motion, and he knew it was just a matter of time before he was knocked off. Even in the short distance he'd come, he felt the beam rotating faster than before.

Maneuvering cautiously because he figured he would have only one chance to do it right, he eased his body off the beam until he was hanging beneath it and facing the stairs, his arm clasped tightly around the beam. Below was the bottomless abyss, and his mouth went dry as he imagined what it would be like if he should lose his grip. Down and down and—no, he wouldn't, he told himself. Blessing depended upon him.

Gently he swung his body forward, then back, and forward again in a gradually increasing arcing motion. When he judged he was close enough, he kicked his legs upward in an effort to wrap them around the beam. He missed. He tried again and got closer, his toes striking it. Again and again he tried, once catching his heel momentarily on the beam, but slipping off before he could wrap his legs around it. Once more he dangled. His arms were tiring fast, his palms sweating. He must make it soon before his hands slipped.

He tried again, swinging his legs up, and this time he was successful. His legs hooked around the beam, he paused to rest. In the past, he certainly had not been accustomed to this sort of physical exertion, and he smiled, thinking of Soong's expression if the old general should see him now. He shifted his arms and legs, then inched forward. Not a dignified position, but the only way he saw of getting across.

Finally he reached the edge of the stairs. He took a deep breath, released one hand and wiped the sweat from his eyes. Then gripping the beam with both hands again, he let his legs drop. He crept closer and carefully probed for a step with one hand. When he finally touched the riser, he grabbed it, then with all of his strength pulled himself slowly up and over the beam, using his legs to lever himself upward.

Ty-Sun sprawled at the base. His legs and arms throbbed painfully from the unaccustomed use. Closing his eyes, he tried breathing more evenly, thankful he'd made it. Quite an accomplishment, he observed smugly, for a man who a year before beckoned with one hand to a servant when he wished a cup of wine or food.

But one part of him nagged relentlessly and uncaring for his triumph. What would he do when he'd rescued Blessing—provided she was here—and they faced the stairs again?

Inwardly he moaned. He would think about that only when they made it back here. In the meantime, he must find her first.

❧— *19* —❧

Ty-Sun paused for breath on the hundredth step. He gazed downward, then away because he could still see nothing but darkness that only reminded him the staircase had no railing. If he got dizzy and started falling, he could clutch nothing except another step.

The only sound during his ascent had been the rasping of his own breath in his ears and his footsteps echoing on the metallic surface. Even now he heard them still ringing faintly and waited until they died away before he resumed climbing.

As yet he'd found no door or other hints at any rooms. Did the staircase simply spiral all the way up to the tree's top? If so, what would he find? Blessing? The Enemy? Both—or neither?

The steps appeared to be narrowing as well, and he took more care as he negotiated them. He didn't want to slip, then tumble down the steps or off them. Either way, it would be fatal.

Several dozen steps up something caught his attention—a small platform on the right with a closed door. He examined the door that was as black and solid-looking as the wall. Holding his sword in one hand, he opened the door cautiously to find a small room and equally empty as the other one outside.

How puzzling, he thought. Apparently there was no way out of the room except the door through which he'd come, and he went back to the platform. More climbing was in order.

Another hundred steps up or so, he found another platform, this time on the left. Another door led into a room as small as the other one, but this time the room itself opened onto a corridor that arrowed straight ahead. Here he found some light, a faint yellow-grey radiance, and when he ran a finger down the wall he felt a slimy dampness on his skin.

It must be some moss or mold growing there that produced the faint light.

He didn't know if it was poisonous, so he quickly rubbed his hand clean and walked down the corridor, his steps muffled in the moss underfoot.

The air circulated sluggishly and smelled of moisture and rot and something else vaguely familiar and unpleasant that he couldn't name. Every so often he paused to listen, but only once heard a faint echo like the clanging of metal from far away. He waited to see if someone appeared, but after a few minutes when no one showed up, he went on his way.

The corridor now angled to the left and the right, and he approached each semi-curve with caution. He never knew what might be on the other side.

He considered it odd, too, that he hadn't seen anyone, not a single guard yet. Were the only guards at the foot of the tree? The Enemy must be very confident that no one could break in.

And where in all of this was Blessing? He wished he would find her soon. If she's here, he thought sadly. She must be, he told himself. He'd come too far for her not to be. He whispered her name aloud, the sound giving him strength.

He was about to retrace his steps when he saw a room ahead. He must investigate. He stepped into the room, saw another door and went through that.

He was back at the spiral staircase only this time opposite the door he'd entered.

Blessing raised her head from her forearms where it rested, blinked because she had been asleep, and gazed around in the darkness. She was bewildered. She'd been dreaming about her father chasing her, but then she thought she had heard someone whisper her name.

She listened, heard nothing, and assumed it had been in her dream.

Which, of course, meant nothing.

The voice sounded vaguely familiar, too. Or was it? If it were, whose was it?

There!

She heard the vague sound again, this time fainter, almost as if it were in her head, or it was moving away from her. It was definitely someone calling her name. But that couldn't be right. After all, she was alone, alone in the darkness. No one knew where she was. She waited, but only silence answered.

Something slimy swung across, slapping him in the face, and he batted it away with his free hand. The slimy thing crunched underfoot, and he glimpsed what resembled a snail dangling on a long thread. He grimaced and continued up the black staircase.

He found another platform, another corridor, but here he found something unlike before. To either side were wooden doors with small openings toward the top barred with metal slats.

Cells, he thought.

He checked the first one on his left and saw a Roman Catholic priest, hardly more than a boy really, kneeling in filthy straw before an inverted wooden crucifix. His habit lay in strips around him, and his slender back was red with lash marks. His genitals had been hacked away then crudely cauterized. The boy whimpered, then muttered to himself as he rubbed his body against the cross, his narrow face and pale blue eyes mad.

Frowning, Ty-Sun crossed to the next cell.

Here he found a woman of considerable age, upon whom he could see the markings of long-ago beauty. A brand had been burned deeply into the pale flesh of her forehead, and the wound still seeped, the blood and pus dripping onto her neck and chest. Even more horrifying were her lips which had been sewn together with heavy black thread that zigged crudely through the tender flesh.

He rattled the door, trying to open it, but the stout wood wouldn't budge. She raised her eyes, but she did not see him.

At her feet in the bloodied straw sprawled a cat, now long dead, its fur matted, and maggots crawling on the carcass.

He turned away in disgust. What madness was this? he asked himself as he watched the woman. Were these prisoners of the Enemy, those who had somehow defied him? Or were they once loyal followers, now being punished for some infraction?

The next compartment contained the body of a girl no older than eight years. Her healthy, pink skin had been flayed in narrow strips and left coiled beside her. How could anyone do such a terrible thing?

Weeping, he passed cell after cell filled with similar atrocities. Some prisoners were dead, their bodies bloated with black flies buzzing around them or infested with maggots. Others would soon meet death.

He reached the end of the corridor with its horrifying rooms and could go no farther. He retraced his steps back to the stairway, trying to push those awful images from his mind.

With each step now he felt as if his body increased in weight, as if his boots were lined with lead. Slower and slower he went, then abruptly he reached a platform enclosing the stairway, and as he stepped out onto it, something sinuous wrapped itself around him and squeezed hard.

❧— 20 —❧

Ty-Sun struggled against the tightening grasp, but could not free himself. He was slowly being squeezed to death, and he knew it was only a matter of time until the thing had wrung his last breath from him. He hadn't caught a glimpse of what attacked him, and now he twisted his head around so he might see.

He paled. The creature holding him was a man-sized centipede—long and loathsome, its shell a strange golden color—one of the Five Venomous Animals feared and despised by all in his country.

The centipede had wrapped its sinuous body around Ty-Sun's body, pinning his arms against his sides, where Dragon's Tongue, still clasped in his hand, hung useless. If he could just break loose, he might have a chance, small as it might be.

Damp soil clung to the fine hairs on the legs of the creature that sprouted from each segment of its body. Those multiple legs embraced him in a deathlock, while the creature's grotesquely oversized head bobbed only a hand-span away from his. Its long antennae waved slightly, and two pairs of fierce black mandibles opened and snapped shut. The first pair of legs behind the head ended in hooked claws, that now clicked ominously and seeped a green poison.

Ty-Sun turned his head as the nauseating odor swept across him. It reminded him of the smell of the grave, of blindly crawling maggots in newly spaded dirt. Of his own death now facing him.

His stomach heaved as he choked back bile. As the creature's body undulated against him, its barbs at the base of its legs pushed into him, tearing his clothes and his skin.

He feared it might not kill him outright, but instead simply toy with him and injure him fatally, then leave him to die slowly and agonizingly with its poison coursing through his body.

What could he do? He couldn't raise Dragon's Tongue, much less use it to kill the creature. He could always throw himself down the stairs, hoping the tumble would kill the centipede, but doubtless he would die as well—and there was that abyss to consider. He didn't want to end up there.

The centipede dragged Ty-Sun's head closer to its poisonous claws.

Suddenly Ty-Sun flung himself across the platform. The creature shrilled noisily, and its legs clamped harder onto its captive. He slammed into the black wall, then spun around so the centipede's slender body was between his back and the wall. He flung himself backward, and once more the centipede made a sound, almost one of pain.

He ground his body against the wall, smashing and slamming against the black hardness. Then he relaxed a little and once more rammed backward, only shifting a little this time so he might further damage another part of the creature's body.

Again it howled as a yellowish ichor dripped down the backs of his legs, pooling at his feet. Good. It was injured.

While Ty-Sun was attempting to crush the centipede, he also struggled to loosen his sword arm. Finally, damaged, some of the centipede's legs weakened and released their tight grip, and his arm broke free. He hefted Dragon's Tongue, slicing behind him. Another shriek, and gouts clung to the steel and to him.

Ty-Sun wrenched himself away from the centipede and turned, squarely facing it. Its body was damaged inside and out. Although it could barely stand, it continued seeping poison, and even as he braced himself to attack it once more, the creature struck, thrusting its mandibles toward him. He leaped aside only at the last moment as he heard the acute sound the jaws made as they snapped and missed him. He swung Dragon's Tongue high and sliced through the creature.

Again and again he hacked at it, and finally the top half toppled over, falling against him. Repelled, he pushed it away and it edged toward the abyss. One leg reflexively gripped Ty-Sun, and he cut away at it until free.

It was dead at last. He wiped the thing's noisome blood from his face with his sleeve, then studied the platform. He'd had no chance to do so before the centipede attacked.

The stairway continued upward as far as he could see, and here there were two doors—one to the left, another to the right of the stairs.

Which was he to take?

The right this time, he decided. Past the open doorway he followed a narrowing corridor cautiously. He didn't desire being surprised by any more unpleasant things again. Green and blue-brown mold and fungus grew profusely on the damp walls here, and occasionally spores burst out from the growths in showers of black and white as he passed.

He held his breath then so he would not inhale the spores, which he little doubted were poisonous. Brilliant orange and yellow and red toadstools and mushrooms sprouted from the floor, and many he did not recognize. He had no doubt that they would prove quite fatal if he were so foolish as to sample even one. This must have been the centipede's lair, and once more he shuddered at the memory of the creature.

The floor rose at a slight angle, and he suspected he must be growing close to the top of the tree now. Surely he would find her soon, if she were here at all. And if not—

Ahead, around a curve in the hall, he caught a glimpse of something light. He paused to grip his sword more tightly then stepped forward to see what new surprise awaited him.

A window.

It was the first he'd seen since entering the tree, so he approached it cautiously. After all, it might just be another trick.

However, it seemed to be just a window with glass in it and a blue-painted frame.

He looked out the window and saw a great expanse of trees, beyond them huge mountains. That must still be Bohemia, he thought. He shifted on one foot, glancing toward the left, and could see the bright blue of the sea he and his friends had left far behind.

How could that be possible? he asked himself. The coast lay hundreds of *li* away—too far away to see even from this great height. Puzzled, he shifted his eyes to the right, and his heart thundered in his chest. Was that the Willow Garden he glimpsed momentarily with greyness settling fog-like about its borders? He thought he saw the Wall of Living Stone, but then he blinked, and the image was gone.

Far to the north he saw something black. As he leaned forward, to see better, he knew that must be the Black Jade Road for which they searched. But how far away was it? Close enough to be seen from this tree, but that didn't mean it was within easy riding distance. And could such things be judged accurately in these circumstances?

He scowled as he left the strange window. He couldn't

believe anything he saw from it, he told himself, and forced his mind to shift from the image of the Willow Garden.

Now the corridor narrowed so much he was compelled to turn sideways, and at the end he discovered a tall ladder. Testing the rungs, he found them solid enough and began climbing carefully. Far above his head the ladder drew up through an open area. What would he find? There was only one way to find out.

He poked his head cautiously through. Nothing attacked him or menaced him which was a good sign. It wasn't as narrow as below, and he could operate more easily. Strange now, because he faced still another corridor. Hadn't he reached the tree's top by now? Perhaps not, although he really thought so. Yet, everything had proved topsy-turvy since he entered the strange black tree. Why did he expect it to make sense now?

He padded softly down the corridor, then stopped abruptly. He sensed Blessing close by now, and he closed his eyes, imagining her sweet smile once more. He stretched out his hand to caress her cheek, then dropped his arm and opened his eyes.

Guards were posted around her, he sensed.

He took a deep breath, preparing himself for another battle. He was growing weary fast, and doubtless the Enemy counted on that. He would find the strength, though, for Blessing.

He crept forward, one slow and silent step at a time, and then came to a bend in the corridor. He paused, gripped Dragon's Tongue firmly, and stepped around the corner.

He saw a barred door, protected by two guards. They resembled men; that is, their bodies were human, but their heads were those of cobras. Emerald pebbly skin drew tautly across a narrow skull, and crimson slashed the full hood. Their eyes were ovoid and yellow with a narrow

black slit in the center. Twin tongues flicked out momentarily then withdrew as the two guards whispered to one
another. They wore black and green uniforms belted by
twisted silver; at their sides hung sword scabbards and
daggers.

Too late to retreat; they had seen him. He imagined he
saw those reptilian lips twist into a smile, and then the
guards withdrew their swords, the sound sibilant in the
corridor.

Two against one. He'd faced worse odds than this before;
still he did not care for it. He knew he couldn't use magic
now in this place of the Enemy. He suspected it would
backfire on him. Murmuring a prayer, he raised Dragon's
Tongue then rushed the guards, who were unprepared for
such an abrupt action. That was precisely what he had
counted upon.

Ty-Sun slashed at first one guard then the other. He
wanted to wound one intially so he could devote his full
attention to the other. He thrust again at the guard at the left,
steel clanging against steel, then whirled around and hacked
at the second guard, who narrowly missed wounding
Ty-Sun.

The snake-men circled him slowly, and except for the
scraping of metal and the soft thudding of their feet, there'd
been no sound since he'd rushed them. Occasionally the
long, sinuous tongues darted out, an unsettling sight, he
thought, and they produced a hissing sound almost like
words.

Hair prickled against the back of his neck, while he told
himself they were no worse than anything else he'd ever
seen or fought. The Enemy wanted him unnerved, counted
on it, but he wouldn't give the Enemy that satisfaction.

The other one shoved his sword at Ty-Sun, who only
managed to throw himself safely to one side at the last

moment. As he did so, he saw that the sword blade gleamed wetly as did the dagger that the guard clasped in his other hand.

Venom? he wondered and shuddered at the idea. He mustn't get even the slightest scratch or else he would die—before he could even draw another breath.

He stumbled, started falling to his knees, then thrust himself back up onto his feet with one hand and leaped around, thrusting Dragon's Tongue into the side of the first cobra guard. The man hissed then drew back, the deep wound gushing blood.

His sword slammed against his opponent's left hand, and the dagger clattered to the floor. Ty-Sun kicked it out of the way then forced his attention to the second guard rushing him.

He was ready, though, and with all the force he could muster plunged his long sword into the guard's neck then raked it across, sawing through the thick muscles and tendons. The cobra's yellow eyes blinked in surprise, and as the hood collapsed, the head wobbled and fell from the guard's shoulders.

Ty-Sun whirled around to face the living guard, who raised his sword, unmindful of his wound. Steel met steel in a resounding clash. They parried, thrust, withdrew, struck again, then retreated, all the while eyeing one another warily.

How long could the other last? Ty-Sun wondered. He was injured and surely the loss of blood would tire him more quickly now. Yet as the minutes passed, the guard didn't weaken. Ty-Sun gritted his teeth and slipping a little on the bloody floor, once more lunged at his opponent. Dragon's Tongue slid into the guard's arm, caught on the bone. Ty-Sun twisted the sword then ripped it out. The guard screamed as bone fragments and blood spouted from his arm. He collapsed onto the floor, twitched, then was still.

Ty-Sun leaned on his sword and wiped the sweat from his eyes. He had to catch his breath. He stared at the dead guards, then closed his eyes momentarily. A few moments later, he selected one of the guard's daggers, nearly as long as Martin's sword. He would give this to Blessing. From now on, she, too, must carry a weapon.

He approached the door and found it locked as he imagined it would be. He located the ring of keys on one of the bodies then started inserting keys into the door. The sixth one worked.

The wide door opened with a mournful creak.

All he saw beyond the portal was darkness. A smell of fear wafted toward him. What if it weren't her, after all? What if the Enemy had somehow changed her, and she no longer wanted him. What if, what if? He shook his head wildly.

"Blessing."

"Who is it?"

A whisper, hardly that.

"Ty-Sun."

With a small sound she launched herself from that dark cell into his arms. He wrapped his arms around her and clasped her close, feeling her hammering heart, feeling his pound just as hard. She shivered against him but did not cry. When her trembling had subsided, he drew back from her slightly, and with his fingers tilted her chin upward. He stroked her hair, her cheek. She closed her eyes as he kissed her, and her lips were warm against his.

"Thank the Mother you came," she said, her voice muffled against his chest. "How long was it?"

"Days and days. Far too long." He buried his face in her hair.

Finally, she moved slightly. "We shouldn't stay here, should we?"

"You're right. We must leave now before the Enemy discovers you're gone." He gave her the dagger. "This is yours—you may well need it before we leave this hellish place."

She nodded and slipped her hand in his, and hand-in-hand they retraced his steps. She did not speak as they passed the cobra guards or the dead centipede out on the landing. From time to time he glanced at her even though the light was not good. He thought she appeared well, but her face was strained. He wondered what had happened to her during her captivity. Perhaps she would tell him. If she had been harmed, then he had that much more against the Enemy.

As they came down the winding staircase to the first room, he gripped her hand tighter.

"Are you ready?"

"Yes, Ty-Sun."

Her gaze and voice were steady, and he smiled at her. Then they stepped onto the beams.

21

"How long has the emperor been gone?" Vlastenecký asked, tapping his foot nervously. He had been pacing back and forth, and Martin had finally persuaded him to sit a while.

"I'm not sure," Soong replied placidly. "At least an hour or two." During the emperor's absence, Soong checked the piece of bark and counted the days which had elapsed, then calculated how much time remained. Of course, if Ty-Sun did not find Blessing inside this unnatural tree, then all of his computations were rather moot. Still, even if they didn't rescue her, he and Ty-Sun would return and make one last stand in the Willow Garden. It would be all they could do.

"Well," the Bohemian muttered, watching the darkening woods, "I don't like this. It's been too long. Surely he should have returned by now. What can be keeping him?"

"She might not be easily found," Soong said. "Too, if he has to climb to the top of the tree that will take much time; it is no sapling."

"I still don't like it. The silence here makes me uneasy."

Soong nodded in agreement. He was uneasy, too, and now that the afternoon light was fast fading from the sky and leaving the woods in darkness, they must double their watchfulness. If only Ty-Sun and Blessing would return. Then they could be on their way.

"It's too quiet," Martin said. He shifted his sword to the other hand and wiped his damp hand on the front of his shirt.

"It is. I advise that you both stand ready." Soong readied his bow.

"The emperor is gone!" Martin cried.

Soong whirled around. The boy was right; Ty-Sun's body had been lying there a moment before and now—nothing. Was this some trick of the Enemy? He shook his head. What were they to do now?

"Wait." Vlastenecký grabbed Soong's shoulder. "Something's going on at the tree."

Soong looked where Vlastenecký pointed and saw that, indeed, something was happening. He peered through the gloom and blinked in surprise. Was that Ty-Sun down there along with Blessing? Suddenly he understood what had happened. Ty-Sun had proved successful—he had returned alive from the astral plane, bringing the English girl with him.

"Come on, men!" he shouted. "That's the Emperor and Blessing, and they need our help!"

The three men scrambled toward the black tree where the soldiers had already surrounded the couple. Ty-Sun was using Dragon's Tongue against a tall man, while at his side Blessing wielded a much smaller, but just as deadly, weapon.

Martin raised his sword and screamed wordlessly as he charged into combat. Vlastenecký lunged at the nearest soldier while Soong loosened an arrow, and the man in front of the nobleman dropped, an arrow in his chest. Another fell, cut down by Dragon's Tongue, then a second one.

Grimly thinking of his murdered family, Vlastenecký faced the two men who replaced his lifeless adversary. He thrust first at one, then at the other, his weapon blurring with his speed. They exchanged blows and lunges, and the shorter of the pair nearly reached the Bohemian, who leaped back just in time. He injured one in the shoulder then launched himself at the second one. He knocked the soldier down, and they rolled over and over, their blades useless now. Martin bounded forward and stabbed the enemy soldier in the side through his leather armor, rolled the man off, then helped Vlastenecký to his feet. The Bohemian grinned and clapped the young man on his back, then they faced their next opponents.

Ty-Sun felled man after man; yet the enemy soldiers kept advancing. How many were there? Would he and the others never be done with them? He caught Soong's attention momentarily and nodded. He was thankful the old general was so alert.

Looking fierce, Soong let another arrow whistle toward its mark. It struck a man in his thigh, and he cried out then crumpled to the ground.

Blessing's dagger plunged deep within the man slashing at her, and he dropped to his knees then pitched forward on his face. She jerked the dagger out and shuddered when she saw the stained blade. And yet, she thought, these men would have no second thoughts about killing us, as they were trying to prove. Resolutely, she whirled around and attacked the closest soldier who was unprepared for her vigorous assault.

An unholy roar assailed their ears while a few of the soldiers wavered momentarily. The bushes beyond the tree thrashed violently, and then something large and dark loomed there. Several men threw down their weapons and fled, howling into the twilight. The bear lumbered forward and took a swipe at a soldier with his paw. He knocked the man down then sat on him.

Ty-Sun smiled, glad the bear was fine, then turned his attention to his next foe.

Martin feinted then slashed hard to his left as still another man raced toward him, and his opponent howled as the thin blade sliced into his arm. What he hated most about these soldiers was their sheer facelessness. They didn't look truly human, and it seemed all of them possessed the same features as if they'd been cut from the same cloth. It was uncanny; it was ungodly, and he would have crossed himself if he could have spared the time. He deflected his opponent's sword, then thrust his own into the other's chest. The soldier fell with a long, drawn-out shriek.

With mounting horror Martin watched as the corpse began collapsing in on itself, growing smaller and disintegrating until nothing but small black things resembling ants remained. The black things swarmed forward, and without thinking, he stomped on them, trying to kill them. One of them managed to escape and climbed up his boot. He tried to brush it away but missed, and the thing bit him on the hand.

Martin cried out at the pain that was like the thrust of a red-hot iron against his skin and shook the insect off and crushed it under his boot. His hand throbbed, but when he inspected it he saw only a small red mark. It wasn't important right now, he told himself, and went to help Vlastenecký.

A soldier, his armor made of the small bones of babies, leaped in front of Blessing and would have beheaded her with his broad sword if the bear had not roared and pounced on him that very moment. When the bear ambled away, the man did not move. Blessing patted the animal's flank briefly in gratitude then whirled around to face her next foe.

The dead littered the forest floor. Vlastenecký had a mild scratch on his cheek, while Martin had sustained the most serious injury. His hand was now throbbing and swelling so that he could barely hold his sword. Grimly, though, he kept his fingers pressed around the hilt. It was hard to feel the metal guard; his fingers seemed as large as sausages. He watched in horror as the sword slipped from his numb fingers and fell to the ground.

One of the soldiers seeing that leaped toward him, a spear poised to run Martin through. What he hadn't counted on was Soong's arrows. The arrow sang as it sped through the air then buried itself in the man's throat. Blood spurted from his neck, then he toppled over, dropping the spear.

"What's wrong?" Soong shouted over the din of clashing swords.

"My hand . . . something bit it, general, and now I can't hold onto anything. I'll try with my other hand, though."

Martin picked up his sword in his left hand and gingerly hefted its unfamiliar weight then swung it a little. How strange it felt. He lunged at a soldier trying to kill Vlastenecký.

The sword did not work true because his left arm wasn't nearly as strong as the right one, but it managed to do the trick, and he nicked the man. The man, tall and dark with acquiline features, whirled around to see what was irritating him from the back. Vlastenecký ran him through. This last soldier wavered then fell dead to the ground.

"Thank you," Ty-Sun said, taking Martin's hand. The boy flinched a little but said nothing. "And thank you, Lord Vlastenecký."

The Bohemian only nodded and wiped the sweat from his face with his sleeve.

Soong rubbed his eyes. He was tired and hungry but knew they couldn't rest yet. "I think we should leave now before reinforcements arrive. Doubtless the Enemy will have discovered Blessing's gone, and I want to be as far ahead of him as possible."

Ty-Sun nodded, and Martin and Vlastenecký ran to fetch the horses.

Something rustled in the underbrush, and Ty-Sun whirled, weapon ready. A small black and white head poked through the greenery, and Ty-Sun chuckled, relieved it wasn't some new foe.

Martin, leading two horses, spotted the new arrival at once. "Why, it's Mistress Blessing's cat. I never thought we'd see her again after she was captured. Here, puss." He stooped and held his hand out to the cat who approached carefully then licked his fingertips with her raspy tongue.

The cat was far thinner than when they'd last seen her, her ribs plainly showing on her matted sides. Soong found some dried meat in their supplies and fed her. She ate quickly, then purring, rubbed gratefully against his ankles.

"She must have followed her mistress here," Ty-Sun said. "If we could have followed the cat then. Ah well, it all came out right." He paused and frowned. "Where's the bear?"

"I saw him a moment ago," Martin said. He held his hand on his chest.

"Over here," Soong called grimly from one side of the clearing.

A tightness knotting his stomach, Ty-Sun went to where Soong stood.

The bear lay in a great heap, one paw curled around his snout. Six black arrows had pierced his thick fur, and blood seeped from the wounds. Underneath him lay a dead soldier.

Ty-Sun dropped onto his knees and caressed the bear's head.

"Old friend," he whispered and knew the bear was dying.

The bear raised his head, and Ty-Sun saw his eyes were

already clouding over. Blessing knelt beside Ty-Sun and stroked the beast gently, murmuring to him.

"Is there nothing you can do?" Ty-Sun asked.

Tears in her eyes, she shook her head. "He's lost too much blood."

His own pain forgotten, Martin hugged the bear and thanked him for his friendship then, crying openly, walked away.

Ch'u was curled up next to the bear as if he could warm the great beast somehow, and a few minutes later the bear rumbled softly.

"It will be soon," Blessing whispered.

Ty-Sun murmured to him, talking about the beast's many feats and the many adventures they had shared and how much his friendship meant to Ty-Sun and how he was glad he had rescued him in Russland. When he looked down, the bear's massive chest was still.

He felt numb. He had lost another friend, and this upset him more than any other death except Spring Rain's. Many times he had dreamed of the time when they returned to the Willow Garden, the bear with them, and he had known his concubines would pamper the animal once they overcame their initial fear. He had imagined the bear lounging in the sun, watching the goldfish in the lily-strewn ponds, sharing meals with Ch'u and the other dogs and cats. Now the poor bear would never see Ty-Sun's beloved Willow Garden.

"We must bury him."

"We can't, Your Majesty," Soong said. "We don't have time."

Ty-Sun rose to his full height and gazed imperially at the general.

"We will bury him."

"Soong's right," Vlastenecký replied somewhat gruffly. "I don't mean any disrespect, but the bear's rather large, and it will take hours to bury him, and we don't have the time."

"We must bury him," Ty-Sun repeated stubbornly. He crossed his arms, and his expression was faintly unpleasant.

"I suggest," Blessing said, intervening quickly, "that we build a pyre for him. That way the Enemy cannot harm his body even in death. What do you say, Ty-Sun?" She gazed intently at him.

He thought momentarily, then: "That would satisfy me."

Soong nodded. They all dragged branches and sticks to the middle of the clearing. When they had a pile of wood and dried matter standing several feet high, they rolled the bear's body gently onto it with some effort. Ty-Sun murmured a few words over the bear, then Blessing bent down and kissed the animal farewell.

Ty-Sun lit the fire and watched as the flames licked along the wood. When the first flames touched the bear's fur, he turned away.

Soong had already mounted. "Come, Ty-Sun. We haven't a moment to spare."

Nodding, Ty-Sun swung up into the saddle and pulled Blessing up in back of him. The others mounted and quickly left.

Ty-Sun did not speak as they rode, and only once did he look back to see the yellow flames leaping high into the air.

Blessing's arms tightened around him as she laid her cheek against his back.

"Where to, General?" Vlastenecký called over his shoulder some time later.

"To the Black Jade Road."

22

The small band rode north and east all that day and the next, hardly pausing for rest. Occasionally Soong glanced over his shoulder for any signs of pursuit, and that he detected none so far did little to reassure him.

Ty-Sun thought often of the bear, and though he did not speak of the beast, he missed his presence greatly. Even Ch'u seemed to miss his large friend and whimpered from time to time. Ty-Sun tried not to think of how many others they might lose before arriving home.

Martin did not speak to any of them during the next few days, and when they camped that night, he maintained his unnatural silence. Concerned, Blessing checked his hand, although he hadn't complained. The fingers and wrist were swollen as well now, and when she touched the skin, she found it warm.

"It's fevered," she said. "I think there must be some sort of poison in it. You said an insect-like creature bit you?"

"Yes."

"I'm going to lance it, and that way the poison should drain. Then it can begin healing. Is that all right?"

He nodded, swallowing quickly. "Whatever you say, Mistress Blessing."

"What do you need, Mistress?" Vlastenecký offered from beside her.

"Water heated over the fire, a clean rag or two, and a needle. I have the last, I think." She stood up and searched carefully through her small pack of belongings. She found what she needed then returned to the fireside.

Martin trembled, and in the yellow flickering light his face was grey.

"This will hurt," she warned gently as she held the needle in the flames. She sensed his unspoken question. "Generally passing a needle through fire prevents the wound's festering."

"Somehow, it must appease the spirits of the air," the Bohemian nobleman said thoughtfully. "'Tis a marvel how she knows these matters."

"A very wise woman indeed, Lord Vlastenecký," Soong agreed.

Soong and Ty-Sun watched her clean Martin's hand, then when the needle fairly glowed, she quickly lanced the bite mark. He yelped, tried to jerk his hand away, but she held on tightly. The wound opened now, and greyish-green pus poured out.

She held his hand over the fire, but not so close to the flames that he would be burned and let the wound drain there. Each time the pus dripped into the fire, the flames sizzled and flickered, and Ty-Sun thought he saw a great shadow there. Finally no pus ran and only a few drops of blood oozed.

Blessing carefully studied his hand. When satisfied, she released it. Martin stared at the red and ugly wound. The puffiness was gone, and for the first time in days he could flex his fingers, however slightly.

She dipped a cloth in the hot water and carefully washed his hand, then she sprinkled some powdered herbs on the hole. He flinched, but did not complain as she wrapped a fresh cloth around his hand as a bandage.

"We must change this daily, and if it should begin seeping, let me know. The herbs are there to help soothe the wound. With luck, you should soon be healthy and whole again." She picked up her things and returned them to her pack.

"You are an amazing healer, Blessing," Ty-Sun said afterward.

She shook her head slightly. "Only sometimes, I fear." She glanced at Martin, now dozing by the fire, the cat lying on his stomach, and drew her fair eyebrows together.

"What's wrong?"

"I'm worried about him."

"But you cleaned the wound out. The poison is gone, isn't it?"

"Yes, from the hand, but I fear some might already have spread to his body. And if that's so . . ." She left the sentence unfinished.

Ty-Sun shuddered at the grim thought. Would he lose yet another friend? Would still another death be added to the horribly long tally for which he was already responsible?

He closed his eyes and not for the first time wished he were once more in the Garden, away from death and danger, away from his grief. Home where there would be no problems at all.

"We're almost to the border of Russland now," Soong told them a few days later, "and that much closer to the Black Jade Road."

Ty-Sun nodded. His thoughts centered almost entirely on the road now; even in his sleep he dreamed of it. What if they could not find it after all this? He could not bear to think of such a possibility. He glanced at Martin, riding to his left. It was evident the boy's pain had come back some time ago, but when Blessing checked the hand that night, the wound was healing. She gave Martin an herbal drink, and he slept long and soundly, but he did not get any better.

The next day Marin rode only vaguely aware of being in the saddle. He thought he'd been tied there so he wouldn't fall out, but he couldn't be sure. In fact, he didn't care. He was too weary to talk, to glance around, to even think.

The numbness in his arm was spreading, seeping through his body with each breath, each beat of his heart, and he knew that within days, perhaps even hours, he would be dead. He tried to tell his friends, but his mouth wouldn't open.

During the daylight hours, he dozed fitfully. When they camped at night, he slept, strange dreams assailing him. Sometimes he was serving Lord Elphinstone and sometimes it was the emperor, and sometimes he was with Spring Rain. Once he woke, and seeing Ty-Sun nearby, struggled to speak.

"You must . . . leave . . . me," he said, the effort exhausting him. Colored dots swarmed before his eyes, and he wanted to close them and sleep but knew he couldn't. Not yet. Not now. He must stay awake.

"Leave you?" Ty-Sun asked. "Nonsense, Martin, we'll do no such thing."

Martin shook his head violently, or so it seemed to him, and yet to Ty-Sun the movement was barely perceptible. "Leave me now. Slow you . . . down. I'm . . . dying. Leave me."

"No. That is enough of that."

Ty-Sun strode away, but not before Martin saw the tears in the other man's eyes.

The young man slept the rest of the night, and in the morning, he was the coldest he had ever been in his life. He couldn't remember ever being warm. He tried looking around, but he couldn't. His arms and legs wouldn't move nor would his head. He opened his mouth to speak, but no words came.

He saw Blessing bending over him, and she was holding a cup of warm liquid, carefully guiding him as he drank it. At least, he thought he was drinking, but he didn't remember swallowing. She was talking gently to him now, but something was wrong with his ears because he couldn't hear. He knew she knew that, too, and that it saddened her as well.

Tears dimmed his vision, and he was growing colder by the heartbeat. He was so numb he couldn't even shiver. Martin wanted to cry. When would he see Lord Elphinstone again? And what about Spring Rain? No, one part of him reminded, she was dead.

Tears flowed then, and first greyness, then blackness, enveloped him.

"He's dead," Blessing said. She caressed the boy's face gently, wiped away the tears he had shed in the last moments of his life.

Ty-Sun did not speak, but instead turned away to help Soong and Vlastenecký dig Martin's grave. They would bury him, and someday if possible, return to bring his body back to the Willow Garden.

The grave was too shallow for Ty-Sun's liking, but when they had interred Martin's body, they piled rocks upon the gravesite to mark it and to keep animals from it.

Ty-Sun could not speak, so Soong spoke of the boy and his courage, and when they were finished, they left this place of sadness.

23

Summer ended as they crossed the grass-covered steppes of Russland, and by now the band of four journeyers was pushed to the point of exhaustion.

In the days since Martin's death, they had still not been pursued by the Enemy, and yet they were not reassured by this. Soong reminded them to remain always on guard, and even at night they slept slightly.

Autumn arrived briefly as the leaves on the trees turned the color of flames, and the air was pungent and fresh, but then brisk winds blew the leaves away and the temperature plummetted. Soon Ty-Sun and the others passed into land where the trees grew fewer, the ground more rocky as they headed toward mountains. Here they encountered occasional rains, cold and dreary, that pounded down upon them so severely they were forced to camp in the shelter of a cave or mountainside for days on end. Only when the rain became a drizzle would they set off through the mud once more.

They still took turns keeping watch during the night, but often Soong warned them not to maintain a fire. He was only too aware of how easily it could be seen on this great flat expanse of land.

In a few days the first early snowstorm howled out of the

great mountains ahead of them, and they struggled against icy winds. The snow and wind blinded them. Only by using the Orb did Ty-Sun keep them from freezing.

Blessing now carried the cat in a sling across her chest, while little Ch'u remained, shivering, in the last of Ty-Sun's great pockets. He did not see how the animals would survive, but they must. He would not allow anyone else to die.

During the day they spoke little and not at all at night. Each was lost within his or her own dreary thoughts. And now, too, the dreams began.

Soong dreamed of leading his army into battle. Each sensation was as real as if he were truly on the battlefield, and he watched as the hand-selected men in his two divisions, the White Tiger of the west and the Green Snake of the east—all of them like sons to him— rushed to meet the Enemy. He cried out in frustration as the Enemy's army charged forward, surging around his men and cutting them off. One by one those of the White Tiger and Green Snake were slaughtered. He awoke, his cheeks damp with tears.

Vlastenecký dreamed of his wife and children alive once more, but even as he watched, as though from a great distance, he saw those he thought were friends and good neighbors rush into his home and set it afire. He watched helplessly as his wife was slain, her stomach with their unborn child in it cut open, watched as the small children were dispatched as if they were nothing but insects. The oldest boy and girl tried to fight back, kicking and hitting at their assailants, but they, too, fell, blood pouring from numerous wounds. He wept for his family and for himself.

Blessing found herself with her father and her mother, and they were arguing. Or at least her father was. Her mother remained silent, her hands clasped in front of her. He yelled at her, then struck her with the back of his hand.

When her mother rose, protesting at his violence, he hit her again, and she fell, striking her head on the side of the table. Then her father dragged the unconscious woman outside and piled sticks and pieces of wood upon her then lit the small pile. Blessing woke screaming as she saw the terrible flames envelop her mother's living body.

Ty-Sun dreamed of shadows. The Enemy, one moment black, then white, then shifting to grey, darted lithely among the shadows, and sometimes the Enemy wore the face of Blessing, sometimes Soong's, sometimes that of Madame Shou, the old dragon. Ty-Sun ran after the Enemy, who darted in and out of the shadows, but Ty-Sun could never catch him, and his anger and hate grew. Once in a while he caught a glimpse of a black dog running at the Enemy's side, and Ty-Sun knew the dog's true identity. Ty-Sun vowed he would kill both the dog and his master for what they had done to his friends and servants, and whenever he thought this, he heard silvery laughter in his mind. The Enemy, he knew, but he would not let that deter him. He would defeat the Enemy because he was a great magician, he commanded more power than the Enemy.

Once again the Enemy laughed, a sound that disgusted Ty-Sun.

Each night the dreams visited them, and they slept little. In the day they struggled onward. The horses were exhausted, barely able to carry their burdens, and finally Soong knew they must let them go. The animals could no longer work for them, and he would not see them die. They freed the horses then rearranged the few remaining supplies and started walking.

Every day it stormed worse and worse, the biting snow piling up in staggering drifts around them, and the wind blew so hard they were forced to keep their heads down so they could breathe.

"We'll never make it to the road this way," Soong shouted over the screaming wind while Ty-Sun merely nodded.

Night and day became one, with no distinction between the two. The days were as dark as the nights and just as cold. When they rested, they huddled around the Orb to keep warm; yet they were never comfortable, never warm enough.

Finally, on the worst day of the unnatural storm, Ty-Sun risked raising his head briefly to look around. What he saw confirmed his worst suspicion. They were lost in the midst of this swirling white. He said as much to Blessing who shook her head.

"No, we're not." And drawing away from him, she began singing. Her voice carried over the sounds of the wind, drifting far away, and as the minutes passed, she continued singing.

"It's no good," Ty-Sun said sadly.

From far away a baying answered. As Blessing sang, the baying grew closer. Ty-Sun glanced at her quizzically, but all she said was, "Help is on its way."

Suddenly dark shapes appeared through the snow, and Ty-Sun saw they were surrounded by dozens of wolves. His hand clasped the hilt of Dragon's Tongue, but she touched his arm.

"No, don't. They've come to help us."

She approached the leader of the pack, a thin, old male with a tattered ear, and sang softly to him. She leaned forward and stroked his grey fur then turned to the others who watched in astonishment.

"He said to follow them."

Ty-Sun stumbled after her as did the others. At times it was nearly impossible to see the wolves in the blowing snow, but each time the animals paused for the humans to catch up. Hours passed; still the wolves led them through the storm.

Gradually Ty-Sun noticed an easing of the wind and of the driving snow, and wondered if the storm were ending. Or maybe it would soon renew itself, only this time more fierce than ever.

Ahead in the dim light, he saw something long and black and gleaming. He squinted, blind for so long by the snow, then gave a great shout.

"The road is ahead!"

Soong cheered raggedly, and they started running toward it. When they had nearly reached the road, Soong paused. The wolves were gone, their task having been accomplished.

And Vlastenecký was gone, too.

Ty-Sun whirled around and looked for the nobleman but saw nothing. He doubled back and searched the white expanse just covered and kept calling Vlastenecký's name, but no one answered. Grimly he knew the man was gone for good, having no doubt fallen by the way during the storm. Another death, another toll for him.

Blessing took him by the arm and brought him back to the general.

"Well, we've finally found the road," Soong said, "or at least the wolves showed us the way."

Ty-Sun nodded numbly and allowed himself to be led to the Black Jade Road.

"Look." Blessing pointed westward.

With mounting horror they saw darkness roiling toward them, swallowing everything in its path. The entire sky and earth had been enveloped by night; not even the stars gleamed through the Darkness.

"The Enemy," Soong whispered.

Even as they watched, an arm of the darkness reached

the road to the west. Some of it crept northward as if seeking to cut their escape off. If they waited much longer, they would be swallowed up by the darkness and what horrors lay within it.

"Come," said Soong, taking Ty-Sun's hand and Blessing's. "We must hurry. Our time is nearly done, but we'll soon be home."

Ty-Sun stepped onto the Black Jade Road, and as a great tingling surged through his body, he glanced back at the darkness, and he knew in his heart that he and his two friends would return to the Willow Garden to defend it. It was only a matter of time.